Let's Go Fishing!

Let's Go Fishing!
A BOOK FOR BEGINNERS

BY GERALD D. SCHMIDT

Illustrated by Brian W. Payne

ROBERTS RINEHART, INC. PUBLISHERS

This book is dedicated to the memory of Ron Tollefson. He was a friend and a fisherman.

Text copyright © 1990 by Gerald D. Schmidt
Illustrations copyright © 1990 by Brian W. Payne
Published by Roberts Rinehart, Inc. Publishers
Post Office Box 666, Niwot, Colorado 80544
International Standard Book Number 0-911797-84-X
Library of Congress Catalog Card Number 90-62933
Printed in the United States of America

Contents

"Give me a fish and feed me for a day. Teach me to fish and feed me for a lifetime." —An old saying

Preface

This book is an introduction to fishing. Many people want to fish but do not know where to begin. For children and adults the many kinds of tackle, bait, fish, and lures seem to be very confusing. This book answers the basic questions of how to fish and what kind of equipment to use for what kind of fishing. There is information on how to clean and care for your catch and even some basic ways of cooking the fish you keep.

But fishing is not always easy. It can be very frustrating at times, but it is a challenge that can be met by everyone who has patience and the willingness to learn some basic and interesting techniques.

This book covers freshwater fishing in North America. Saltwater fishing is every bit as much fun, but usually different tackle and techniques are used. Because successful fishing in the ocean involves almost entirely different species of fishes and methods of catching them, this small book cannot include this fascinating aspect of angling.

Sports fishing is the most popular form of recreation in the United States today, and thousands more people are beginning to learn it every year. Fishing is popular among everyone, young and old, male and female. In fact, as many girls as boys enjoy it, so when I use the word "fisherman" I really mean everyone. Even many handicapped persons can enjoy fishing. Its popularity lies in the fun of not only the catching of fish but, just as important, in providing the opportunity to get outdoors and enjoy what you see and feel. Some of the best fishing is in beautiful places, like the national parks. However, anywhere you fish you can learn about nature and the wonderful relationships between all animals and plants.

Fishing teaches good sportsmanship, how to get along with other people, and to respect nature and even the very fish you are trying to catch. By taking the time to learn about fish, what they eat, and where they live, you will spend many happy hours discovering a world that may be entirely new to you.

Introduction

When I was a little boy I used to walk to a nearby lake to go fishing. With a fishing rod in one hand, a can of worms in the other, and a hat to keep the hot sun off my head, I walked quickly in hopes the fish were biting that day. My favorite place was a wide ditch that wound its way through cattails just before entering the lake. Fish liked to swim up into that ditch because there was lots for them to eat there. I would cast my line into the slowly moving water and hope one of those fish would find my bait. Today, many years later, I still can remember the thrill of seeing my bobber jiggle, and begin to float away as an unseen fish tried to eat the worm and swim away with it. I always felt proud when I brought bullhead catfish and carp home for the family to eat.

I also watched wide-eyed as snakes, turtles, birds, and other wild things accepted me as part of their world and went about their business as if I were not there. This was my introduction to biology, a science I have enjoyed all of my life as a biologist and teacher . . . and as a fisherman.

But I also had a lot of problems. I didn't know how to tie knots that would not come loose, so I lost a lot of fish and hooks. I did not know how to care for the fish I caught, so sometimes they spoiled in the hot sun and could not be eaten. Once when I had a bite, I jerked so hard that I broke my fishing rod right in half because the fish was very big.

When I was growing up there were no books to help young people learn how to fish. That is why I have written this one. By now I have fished in many parts of the world for many kinds of fish. But the basic techniques I use today are the same ones I learned at the beginning. Because I did not have much help from experienced fishermen, it took me a long time to learn. I hope this book will help you to learn faster how to catch fish than I did. But part of the fun is discovering new ways for yourself. You will continue to do this all of your life, and have a wonderful hobby that will not only feed you but give you much pleasure.

Gerald D. Schmidt
Greeley, Colorado
August 1990

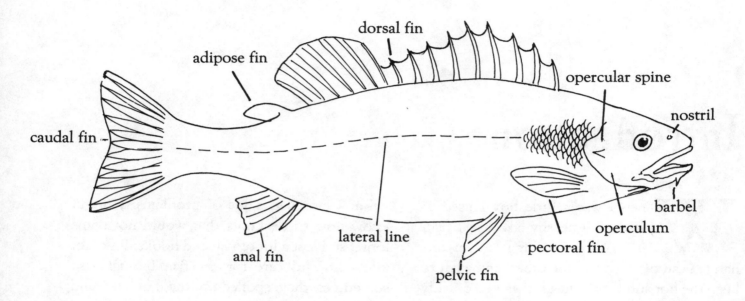

Figure 1-1. Names of the outside parts of a fish

1. Kinds of Fish

There are over 80,000 kinds of fish in the world. Most live in the oceans, but a great many are found in the United States and along its ocean shores. We cannot discuss all of these, because most are small species of no interest to the fisherman. Even among those kinds of fish that offer sport and food to fisherman, only a few of the most common and available species will be discussed in this book. These fish are the ones most beginning fishermen are likely to catch. The basic parts of the outside of the fish are shown in figure 1-1.

Some of these fish are not considered very great prizes by some anglers, while others are highly treasured. And yet, what pleases each fisherman is what is important.

Most kinds of fish prefer to live only in certain kinds of water, while others may be found in several locations. It is important for the fisherman to know where each kind of fish is most likely to be found. For example, we would not expect to catch a sunfish off a pier in the ocean or a shark in a farm pond! Now I will tell you about several kinds of fish that are popular in the United States. Others may exist where you live.

Fish in Ponds and Lakes

Sunfish. There are many kinds of sunfish, such as bluegill (fig. 1-2), pumpkinseed, green, and orange-eared sunfish. Most are found only in fresh water, although some are found in slightly salty water, such as the Chesapeake Bay. These short, flat fish are eager biters, fun to catch, and delicious to eat. They can be caught on many kinds of bait, flies, and lures.

Crappie. This silvery, big-mouthed fish (fig. 1-3) is a friend to fishermen throughout the freshwaters of North America. When you can find them, they are eager eaters, so are easy to catch. Not much larger than sunfish, they are easy to clean and are great to eat.

Freshwater bass. Large-mouth (fig. 1-4) and small-mouth (fig. 1-5) black bass actually are big sunfish. They are much harder to catch than the smaller species, so they are considered real gamefish. They mostly eat smaller fish, frogs, and crayfish. To catch them, the angler must use larger, more active baits or lures.

Figure 1-2. Bluegill sunfish

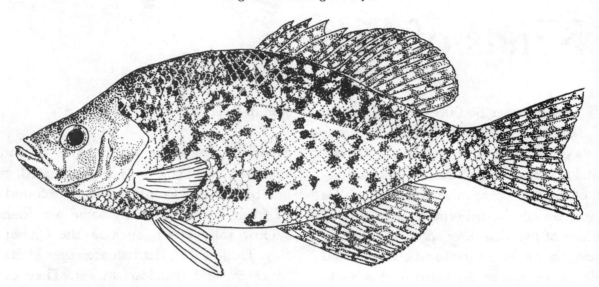

Figure 1-3. Crappie

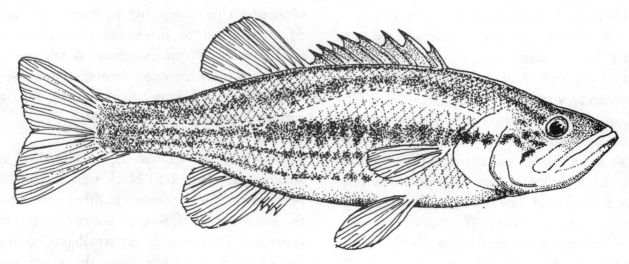

Figure 1-4. Large mouth bass

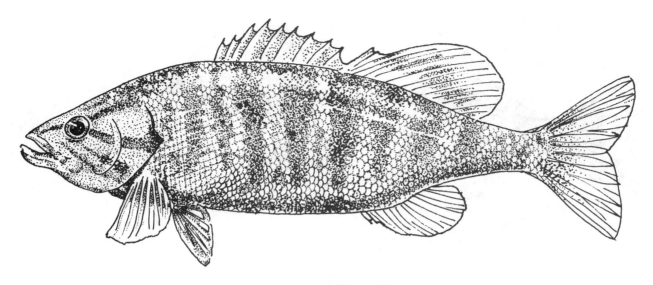

Figure 1-5. Small mouth bass

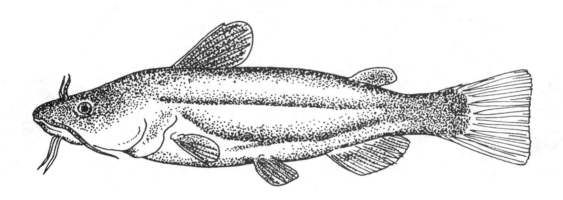

Figure 1-6. Bullhead catfish

Figure 1-7. Yellow perch

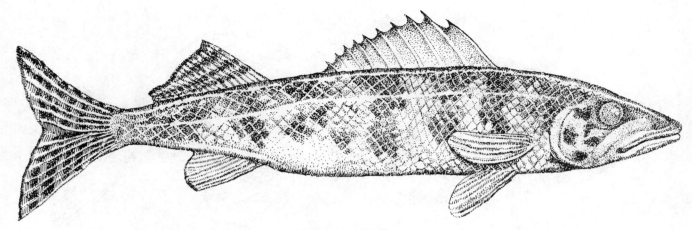

Figure 1-8. Walleye

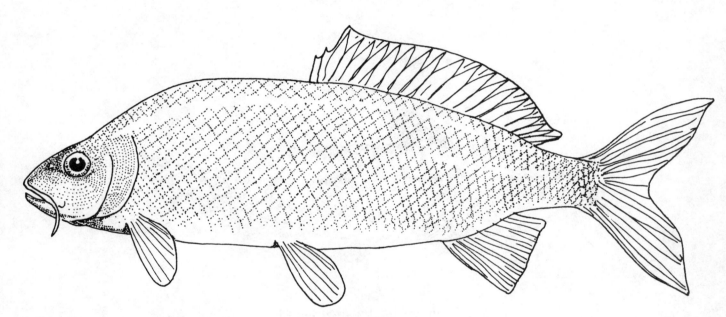

Figure 1-9. Carp

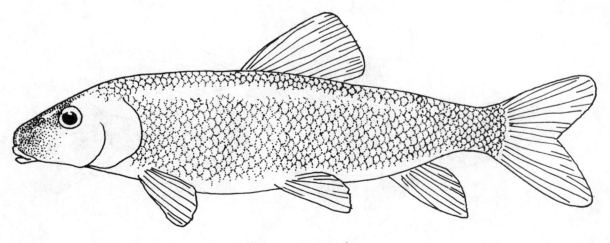

Figure 1-10. Sucker

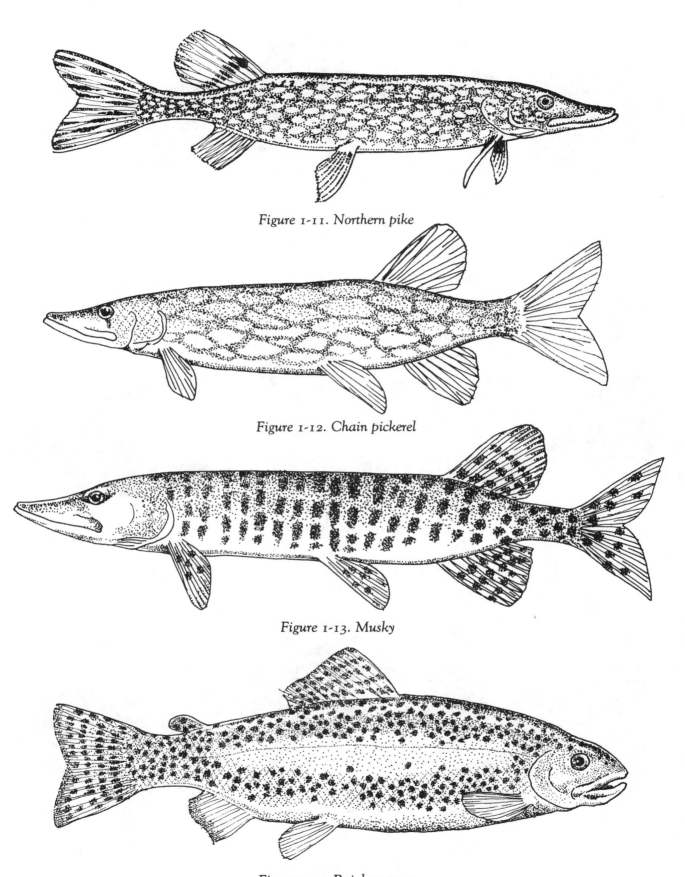

Figure 1-11. Northern pike

Figure 1-12. Chain pickerel

Figure 1-13. Musky

Figure 1-14. Rainbow trout

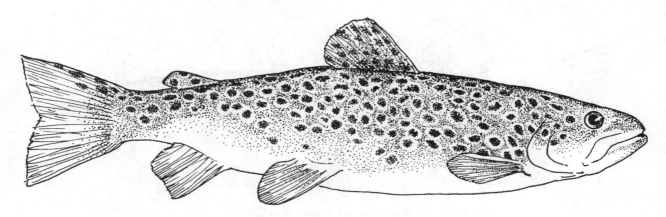

Figure 1-15. Brown trout

Figure 1-16. Cutthroat trout

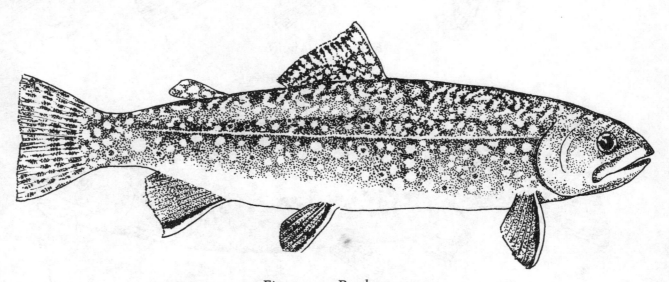

Figure 1-17. Brook trout

Catfish. Like the sunfishes, there are many kinds of catfishes (fig. 1-6). All of them are easily recognized by their lack of scales and by their flat heads with long "whiskers" hanging down. These whiskers, or "barbels," are covered with taste buds that help them find food in muddy water. The most common kinds of catfishes are bullhead, channel, blue, and flathead. Bullheads are the most common of all catfish. They are small, seldom reaching a pound in weight, but they are very easy to catch with bait, such as worms. Catfish are difficult to clean. They must be skinned before cooking. Be cautious: the two spines on the pectoral fins and the one on the dorsal fin are very sharp and are poisonous enough to cause pain for several minutes or hours.

Perch. Many people believe that the perches (fig. 1-7) are the best North American fish to eat. While there are several species, only two— the yellow perch and the walleye—are of great importance to angling. Yellow perch are found from coast to coast in lakes and some rivers. Usually they group together in large numbers, or "schools." When the fisherman finds a school of yellow perch, he may be able to catch a large number in a short time. They prefer to eat small fish, so minnows are usually the best bait for them. A yellow perch that reaches a pound in weight is considered very large. But a giant relative is found in many parts of the United States. This is the walleye (fig. 1-8), often called walleye pike. It's not a true pike, but the name has stuck. Unlike the yellow perch, which has vertical, black bands on its body, the walleye has a slightly speckled green color and its eyes are milky white. Walleyes are much harder to catch than yellow perch. Both species have sharp spines on their fins and are

hard to scale. Skinning is the best technique but takes some practice. Perch have a sharp spine on each operculum that can cut a careless finger, so be careful.

Carp and suckers. Carp are native to Europe and are found in most of the world (fig. 1-9). They are abundant in most waters of North America. Closely related to goldfish, there is only one main species in the United States, although some individuals of this species have few scales while others are totally covered with scales. Although most people think carp are dumb, actually they are rather hard to catch in clear water because of their excellent eyesight. They are one of the most important food fish in the world because they grow to a large size in a short time. Carp have small barbels on each side of their mouth, somewhat like catfish.

Suckers. There are many kinds of suckers (fig. 1-10), but they are also not appreciated by most fishermen. First of all, they are a little funny-looking. They feed on bottom-dwelling organisms and are usually caught by bait fishermen who may become angry because they thought they had hooked a huge trout, or because they have a hard time prying the hook out of the tough mouth of the sucker. Suckers are found mostly in North America in lakes and rivers.

Both carp and suckers are very good to eat, if they are caught in unpolluted waters. They can be cooked in many ways, but care must be taken while eating them, for they have many forked bones between the flakes of tasty, white flesh.

The pikes. Pikes are not found in all of the United States. Mostly they are in northern waters, but they have been successfully introduced into cold waters farther south. They are fierce predators on other species of fish. Most common is the northern pike (fig. 1-11), a fish that looks like and behaves like the barracuda of the tropical oceans. Its mouth has many large, sharp teeth that it uses to welcome in any kind of smaller fish. Because it is greedy and will eat almost any kind of fish that is smaller than it is, usually it is not hard to catch. Or at least to hook—once you have one on your line, hang on!

The pickerel. This fish is a smaller version of the northern pike (fig. 1-12). Its habits and feeding preferences are the same as its bigger cousin, but because it does not grow very large it is not considered to be an important gamefish.

On the other hand, the **muskellunge**, or "**musky**," is the giant of the pikes and is considered the greatest trophy of the freshwater fishes (fig. 1-13). Any angler who catches one can be proud the rest of his or her life!

The trouts. Several species of trout are found in the United States. Most are native to this land but one important one, the German brown, was introduced from Europe.

Trout are among the prized catches of all freshwater fishermen. They are often difficult to catch, which makes them more fun to try for. They are beautiful to look at, and very good to eat. Of the trouts, most anglers seek the **rainbow trout** (fig. 1-14), which not only lives up to its name in beauty, but is an eager biter and often easy to catch. However, they can fool you because while easy to catch on one day, they may ignore all offerings the fisherman has to try the next day. Trying to outguess the

rainbow trout regularly is one of the most fun efforts in fishing. No one has been able to do it yet. Maybe you can?

The German brown trout. The German brown (fig. 1-15) is a great puzzle to fishermen. When small, up to 12 inches in length, they sometimes are easy to catch almost any way. Then, suddenly, when they get larger, they seem to disappear from the rivers and lakes. This is because they stop feeding during the day and begin feeding at night, while the anglers who are in their tents or campers, are discussing the poor fishing of the day! Partly because of this, German brown trout often reach huge sizes, up to 38 pounds! It is difficult and frustrating to fish after dark, and often very cold, but this is when the big brown trout are active. Is it worth the hardship?

Cutthroat trout. Cutthroats (fig. 1-16) are found in western North America. They are very closely related to rainbow trout, and often interbreed with them. They do not have the red stripe down their sides like rainbows, but are yellowish, with most spots located toward the tail, and have a red slash on each side of the throat. Cutthroats sometimes are very easy to catch, while at other times they seem to ignore everything the angler presents to them. They never jump when hooked, as do the rainbows, and are sluggish in fighting, but are among the most beautiful of all our freshwater fishes. Usually, they are found only in high mountain lakes and streams.

Brook trout. Native to northeastern North America, brook trout (fig. 1-17) have been stocked in most cold-water streams and ponds in North America. They are not true trout, but most people do not notice the difference. Instead of spots on their backs, they have worm-like stripes. Their pectoral and pelvic fins are usually very colorful, with white, black, and red stripes. Brook trout are very easy to catch and most people think they are the tastiest of all the American freshwater trouts.

Other kinds of trout and their relatives, such as **lake trout**, **golden trout**, **dolly varden**, and some **salmon** can be found in the United States.

2. Things that Fish Eat

All fish eat other living things and sometimes dead ones as well. Many of their food items are so small we are not likely to see them, and certainly we cannot use them as bait, or even copy them as flies or lures. However, most gamefish food is larger, and some kinds are useful for us to use as bait. There are four main kinds of food that fish enjoy, and we must know what they are so we can know how to fool fish into trying to eat what we have to offer them on our hooks. These four menu items are insects, worms, crustaceans, and smaller fishes.

Insects. Fish like to eat most kinds of insects. Usually they can catch insects that live in the water during part of their lives, then near the water the rest of their short time alive. Before we describe the most common sorts of insects we should know exactly what an insect is. First of all, we should know that adult insects usually do not look much like young ones. For example, look how different a butterfly appears than a caterpillar—yet they are the same animal! Adult insects can be easily recognized in a few ways (fig. 2-1): They always have six legs and their body is in three main parts—a head, thorax, and abdomen. Other similar animals, such as spiders, ticks, and centipedes have different shapes, so are not insects.

Immature insects, on the other hand, may not look very much like their parents. The serious fisherman studies insects, both adults and immature ones, to learn what fish like to eat. Then you can try to fool the fish into thinking that what is on the hook is the real thing!

Some insects, such as grasshoppers, ants, bees, and beetles do not live in the water normally, but may fall in or be blown in by the wind. Fish often like to eat these terrestrial insects (which means land-living). Those that normally live at least part of their lives in water are called aquatic insects, and are among the most important items in the diets of many fishes. A few of the most important kinds of insects are mayflies, midges, stoneflies, caddisflies, dragonflies, and damselflies.

Mayflies. Throughout most of the world, the mayflies are a very important food for fish. Their immature stages, called nymphs or larvae, can be found in pools, lakes, and rivers,

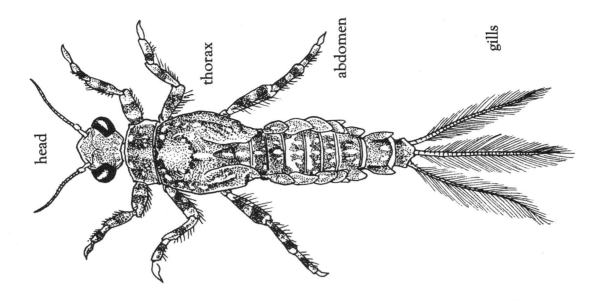

Figure 2-1. *Mayfly nymph, showing basic segments of an insect*

from fresh waters near the oceans to the highest mountains. Mayfly larvae (fig. 2-1) are rather small, flattened animals with six legs and two or three whiskers, or filaments, sticking out the back end of the abdomen. Some burrow into the muddy or sandy bottom of the lake or stream; others live under rocks or hide in aquatic weeds. They may live up to two years in the water before coming out to live in the air. Fish love to eat them at any time. When the larvae try to emerge (come out of the water) fish can catch them easier. They eat them so eagerly that the wise fisherman often can catch many fish using artificial nymphs.

Adult mayflies (fig. 2-2) are beautiful insects, delicate and soft, with two or four wings that they hold straight up when resting, like the sails of a ship. Although their nymphs may live up to two years, the adults live only a few days; just long enough to mate and lay eggs on the water. While laying eggs, mayflies may number hundreds, thousands, or even millions. This usually drives fish crazy, especially trout, which eat them until they are stuffed. During this "feeding frenzy" you can usually catch as many fish as you want if you are fishing carefully.

Artificial flies that are meant to float on the water are called dry flies. Those meant to sink, such as artificial nymphs, are called wet flies. Most kinds or "patterns" of dry flies imitate mayflies.

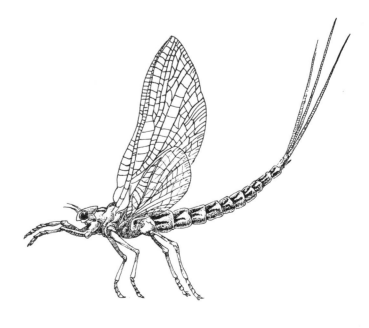

Figure 2-2. *Adult mayfly*

Midges. Many kinds of small insects with only two wings are called midges. Some bite people, but most of them are quite harmless. Midges (fig. 2-3) are among the most common of all aquatic insects, and so are important food for fish. Both the aquatic larvae and the terrestrial adults are favorites of many kinds of fish, especially trout. The larvae (fig. 2-4) look much like small worms and usually are red or green. They live at the bottom of lakes and rivers, and sometimes in soil on land. Shortly before becoming adults they change into a pupa stage, which shows no legs. The pupa (fig. 2-5) wiggles up to the surface of the water, crawls out of its skin, and flies away with its newly-formed wings. While they are doing this, fish can eat them easily. So the fisherman who knows how can use artificial larvae, pupae, and even adult midges to fool fish into biting their hooks.

Some midges look very much like mosquitoes, even though they do not bite people or anything else. I have seen people refuse to leave their car to go fishing because they thought the thousands of midges outside were mosquitoes. So you see how important it is to learn to know one kind of insect from another, both to catch more fish and to protect yourself from those insects that really do bite people.

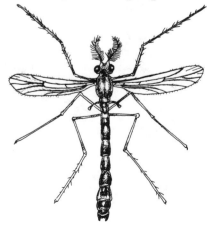

Figure 2-3. Adult midge

Figure 2-4. Midge larva

Figure 2-5. Midge pupa

Stoneflies. These insects are found throughout the United States, especially in cold waters. The larva (fig. 2-6) looks much like the adult except that it has no wings. They range in color from light yellow to green, reddish, and brown. Some get rather large, up to two inches long. The larvae look fierce, but they are quite harmless, and are unable to bite a person. They live on the bottom of rivers and lakes, where they eat tiny plants and animals. When ready to emerge, they crawl out of the water onto rocks or other objects and quickly shed their skins. The adults (fig. 2-7) have four wings that are held flat on top of their bodies when they are resting. They are weak fliers, fluttering over the water while laying their eggs. Their flying so close to the surface of the water attracts fish, and almost drives them crazy, so they eat as many as they can. The lucky angler in this situation may catch many fish, especially trout, by using live stoneflies on a hook or by fishing with imitation stoneflies. Fly patterns (imitation insects) are available from fishing shops, or you can make them yourself it you would like to learn how.

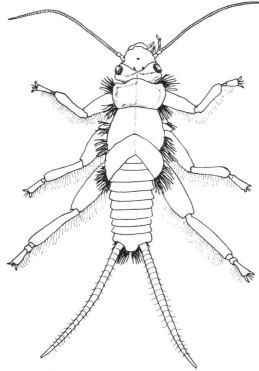

Figure 2-6. Stonefly larva

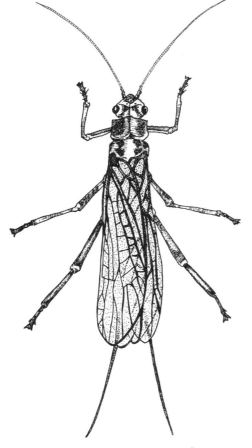

Figure 2-7. Adult stonefly

Stoneflies have different names in different parts of the United States. Adults sometimes are called "willowflies," or "salmonflies," while the larvae are called "hellgrammites" in the western states. Actually, there is a different insect that is correctly called a hellgrammite in some eastern states.

Caddisflies. These little insects have very interesting life cycles. Their larval and pupal stages are entirely underwater, so they are always available as food for fish. They are closely related to butterflies and moths. The larvae look like small caterpillars and the adults look like fuzzy-winged moths. Both are attractive to fish, especially trout, who use them as a major food source.

Most caddisfly larvae live inside little houses, or cases (fig. 2-8), which they make themselves out of silk that they spin from their mouths, and sand, sticks, leaves, or shells that they glue together with their silk. It is interesting that each species has its own housing plan. That is, one kind will use tiny snail shells, another small clam shells, still another grains of sand. Many will cut live leaves of aquatic plants and wrap them around themselves. All of these variations are tricks the insects play to avoid being eaten. The larvae have tiny hooks at the end of their

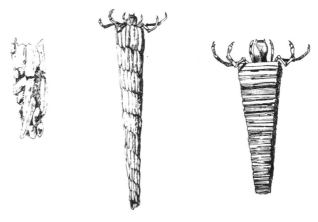

Figure 2-8. Caddisfly cases and larvae

abdomens, and drag their little houses along with them as they search for food. They become pupae in the same cases and emerge as adults (fig. 2-9) that swim to the surface to enter the air. Almost immediately they mate and the females begin laying eggs on the surface of the water. They flutter over the water at great speed. This action attracts fish and they

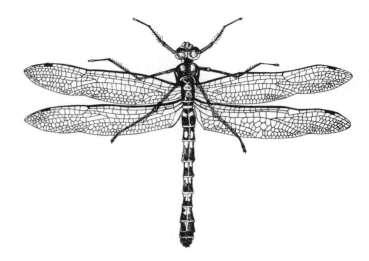

Figure 2-10. Adult dragonfly

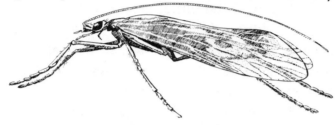

Figure 2-9. Adult caddisfly

begin to attack the insects furiously. Equally furious may be the fisherman who stands in the middle of all of this activity but cannot duplicate the caddisfly's action with his own artificial fly. When the angler learns how to do it he may have more sport than he has ever imagined! The largest rainbow trout I have ever caught (12 pounds) was tricked this way!

Adult caddisflies have long, slender antennae, and hold their wings roof-like over their bodies when they rest. They are attracted to light, like moths, so you usually can catch them around lights outside your house if you want to learn what they look like. Neither larvae nor adults can bite you. Imitating caddisflies is one of the greatest challenges an angler can attempt.

Dragonflies. Most people know dragonflies (fig. 2-10) as those large insects that fly very fast around lakes and streams, eating other smaller insects that they catch. When they finally rest they land on a plant (or the end of your fishing rod) with their wings always held straight out from their body. Actually, adult

dragonflies are seldom eaten by fish because they fly so fast and seldom touch the water. But their larval forms, or nymphs, are choice food for large fish. The nymphs (fig. 2-11) look really fierce, and certainly they are to smaller invertebrates, but to humans they are entirely harmless. They won't bite you. You can catch them under rocks, floating wood, and other things in the water. Usually they are about one inch long. Simply pick them up and put them in a container where they can stay wet. Fish with them just like using worms, described later, in chapter 4.

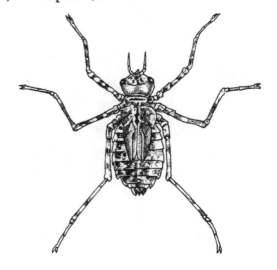

Figure 2-11. Dragonfly nymph

Damselflies. These insects are close relatives to dragonflies, but are much smaller and more delicate (fig. 2-12). They fly slowly and rest often. Every fisherman knows the pretty blue or grey damselfly that rests on his bobber while he waits for a fish to bite. When they rest they fold their wings behind them, unlike dragonflies. Fish get a chance to eat adults sometimes, because the insects fly slowly and usually stay close to the water. But the main source of interest to fish, especially to trout, is the nymph stage. Damselfly nymphs (fig. 2-13) are slender animals that spend their aquatic lives in underwater weeds, eating small invertebrates. They take on the same colors as the weeds, so are green to brown in color. Although fish eat them whenever they can find them, a strange thing happens every spring. In lakes all over the country, thousands, even millions, of damselfly nymphs begin swimming toward shore where they crawl out of the water and become adults. When the the nymphs are swimming, fish can eat them until they are stuffed! I counted over 1,500 damselflies in the stomach of a single trout that still was so greedy that it tried to eat my fly, a rather poor imitation of a damselfly nymph. Damselfly nymphs must taste really good to a fish! It doesn't seem to work very

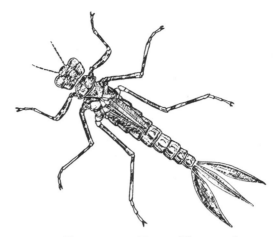

Figure 2-13. Damselfly nymph

well to use a damselfly nymph as bait on a hook, but several kinds of artificial flies do work very well. See chapter 6 for more details.

Worms. Everyone knows what "fish worms" are. And so do fish! The very large "night crawlers" that you can catch in your lawn after dark belong to this group. So do smaller garden worms you can dig out of the ground. And in most bait shops you can buy even smaller "red worms." Nearly all fish love to eat worms, and because worms are so easy to get, they are the most common bait that anglers use. Worms are easy to keep alive for a long time until you want to use them as bait, but a few simple rules must be followed. Never let the soil, or moss, or whatever the worms are in, become dry—this will kill them at once, and do not let them get hot in the sun or in a car in the summer, because heat also kills them. Few things smell as bad as dead worms, and of course, they can no longer be used as bait.

Other kinds of worms such as leeches and very small aquatic species are a preferred diet of fish. Most are not used as bait because they are too small to put on a hook, or are not easily found, so we will not discuss them here.

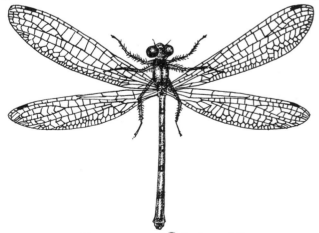

Figure 2-12. Adult damselfly

Crustaceans. These mostly aquatic animals have a hard outer skin like a crust. You are familiar with some crustaceans that people like to eat, such as shrimp, lobsters, and crabs. Even little "roly-poly bugs" that we find in the garden are crustaceans, although they are not usually food for fish. In freshwater, most crustaceans are too small to use as bait or to be duplicated with artificial lures, but some are larger and very useful. For example, crayfish (also called crawdads or crawfish) are rather large animals that look exactly like miniature lobsters (fig. 2-14). They are great food for both fish and humans. Larger fish, such as bass, perch, pike, and trout are very pleased to catch one, so if you are using one as bait or are using a lure to copy it, you may do well.

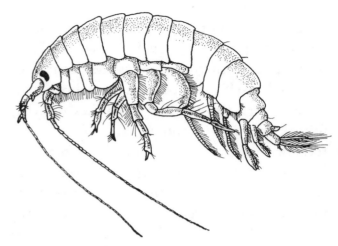

Figure 2-15. Freshwater shrimp

Another kind of freshwater crustacean important to the diet of fish is the freshwater shrimp (fig. 2-15), not closely related to what you eat in restaurants. Also called scuds, there are small species (up to one-fourth inch long) and larger ones (up to one inch). Both kinds of freshwater shrimp are cold water species, and are most important to trout and salmon. Related species of shrimp are abundant in the oceans.

These are among the food items that give trout and salmon their orange-colored flesh and delightful flavor. They are too small to place on a hook as bait, but artificial "flies" have been invented that work very well to fool fish.

Smaller bait fishes. All of us use the word "minnow" to mean a small fish. This is correct, but scientists also use the name minnow to refer to a certain group of fishes, some of which can grow to 100 pounds! Some minnow! A minnow in this book will mean any small fish of many kinds that are common wherever larger fish live. Usually, big fish eat small fish. Some, like German brown trout, eat insects,

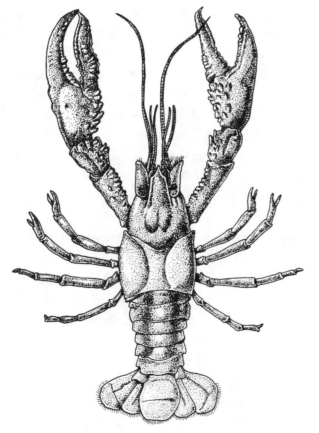

Figure 2-14. A crayfish

crustaceans, and so on until they reach a certain size, then switch over to a diet of almost only smaller fish. So, fishermen who easily catch small brown trout with artificial flies sometimes cannot understand why they never catch big ones. The same can be said for many other kinds of gamefish.

Baitfish usually are used live, but preserved or even frozen ones sometimes are useful. I will discuss how to use them in a later chapter.

3. Kinds of Fishing Tackle and Accessories

There are almost as many kinds of fishing tackle as there are kinds of fish. The tackle you use depends on the kind of water you are fishing in, the kinds of fish you want to catch, and how you want to catch them. Also, it may depend on how much money you can spend, as some tackle is very expensive. However, anyone can catch fish using only the cheapest, simplest equipment.

Most fishermen use the combination of rod, reel, line, and hook. Some fishermen even fish without the rod and reel, holding the line in their hands. So, two things that certainly are needed are a hook and a line. Let's talk about these first, and then about rods and reels.

Hooks. There are many, many kinds of hooks. They come in different sizes and shapes, depending upon what they are used for. Each kind of hook, and each part of a hook has a name. Figure 3-1 shows a typical hook with its parts named. Hook sizes are numbered, with each larger number meaning a smaller hook. For example, a size 10 hook is smaller than a size 8, while a size 12 is even smaller. Really big hooks are numbered just the opposite, with size

1/0 being larger than size 1, and size 2/0 larger than 1/0, and so on. These really big hooks are seldom useful for freshwater fish, however.

The steel wire that hooks are made from may be thick or thin, depending on how the hook will be used. Most hooks are coated with bronze to keep them from rusting, but other metals also are used, such as nickel or gold. Most hooks have very sharp points when you buy them, but some of the very large ones may

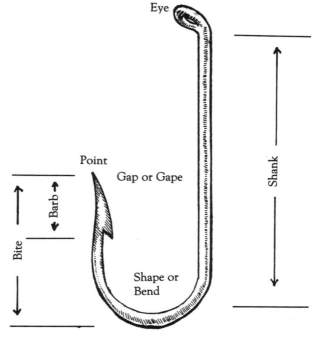

Figure 3-1. A typical hook with its parts named

need to be sharpened even more before you use them. You can buy single hooks to tie on the end of your line, or you can buy them with a short bit of line already tied on. This short line, made of monofilament nylon is called a snell (fig. 3-2). Most beginning fishermen find that a snelled hook is easier to attach to the line. I will discuss how to tie knots later.

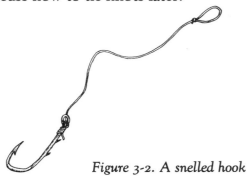

Figure 3-2. A snelled hook

Lines. Fishing lines are of three basic types: monofilament nylon lines, braided bait casting lines and fly lines. Each is used in very different styles of fishing. I will discuss these methods later.

Monofilament nylon lines. Monofilament lines are used with spinning reels in spinfishing. They are made of nylon, which is clear, like glass, so the fish cannot see them. They can be bought in different thicknesses, so some are stronger than others. For example, a six pound line breaks when it is pulled with six pounds of pressure, while an eight pound line is stronger. However, the thicker the line, the shorter the distance you can cast the lure or hook. And remember, when a knot is tied in a line it makes the line weaker at that place because it cuts itself, so a six pound line actually will break at less than six pounds of pull. Monofilament also is used for leader material. A leader is a short length of line between the hook and the main line, like a long snell.

Braided bait casting lines. Braided lines are soft lines made of several threads braided together. Usually, they are used with a special kind of reel, called a bait casting reel, even though artificial lures are used more often than real bait. Handlines are also usually made of this kind of line.

Fly lines. These are very thick, heavy, braided lines that are used in fly fishing (see chapter 6). In this kind of fishing the weight of the line is cast, rather than the weight of the lure.

Rods and reels. These two basic pieces of tackle are used together with line and hook. The kind of rod (or "pole") depends on the kind of reel used. Let's discuss these in the same order as we described the kinds of line.

Spinning rods and reels. Spinning tackle uses the simple idea of a line slipping off of a

smaller. This slows down the speed that the line can have, causing the cast to be shorter. Spinning rods are built to help this problem by having very large eyes first, which gradually get smaller along the rod towards the last eye or "tip-top." These eyes send the line accurately to where you want the cast to go (fig. 3-3). Spinning is probably the most popular way to fish in the United States today.

There are two basic kinds of spinning reels: open faced and closed faced. An open faced reel (fig. 3-4) will let you cast farther because the loops of line coming off the reel are large, and do not rub as hard against the first, large eye on the rod. Closed faced reels (fig. 3-5) have a cap on front with a small hole in it that the line comes out of. But the large loop of line rubs immediately on the edges of this hole and the resulting friction keeps the cast from going as far. Later in the book I will describe how to use these reels.

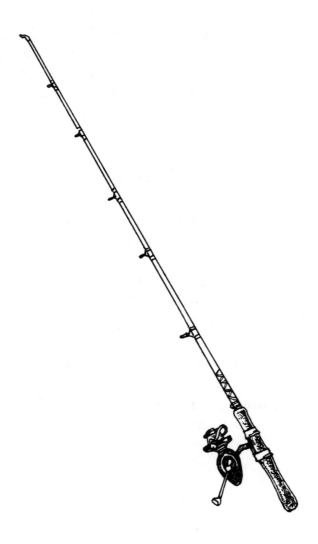

Figure 3-3. A spinning rod and reel

spool. Picture a soda pop can with a line wrapped around it. If you pull the line off the end of the can it will pull off easily. Spinning reels are exactly the same. Two problems are built into this system and cannot be got rid of. First, when the line pulls off, it twists the line. This twist usually comes out when you wind the lure back, however. Second, when the loop of line comes off the reel it is a wide loop, so when it goes into the first "eye" of the rod (eyes are the metal rings that the line flows through along the rod) it is forced to become

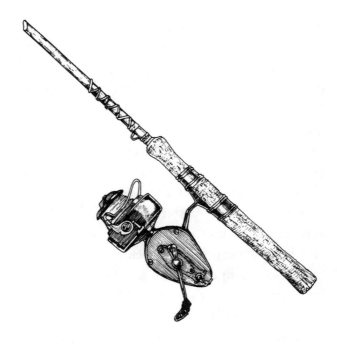

Figure 3-4. An open faced spinning reel

Figure 3-5. A closed faced spinning reel

Bait casting rods and reels. Bait casting tackle (fig. 3-6) is misnamed, because you usually don't use bait with it. Instead you most often cast heavy lures, such as spoons, plugs, or other artificial baits. I'll describe how to use these lures in chapter 5. The main idea is that as the line comes off the reel, the reel's spool spins backwards, unwinding the line. This sounds simple, but really it is the hardest kind of casting, and takes a lot of practice to get it right.

Figure 3-6. A bait casting reel and rod

You see, the reel's spool begins to pick up speed and very soon is spinning faster than the line is going off. In a second or two the line can become very tangled in a mess usually called a "backlash," or a "bird's nest." To prevent this tangling the fisherman uses a thumb to gently slow the speed of the spool while the line is flowing out. It takes a great deal of practice to learn how to do this. When I was a boy I used a rubber weight (instead of a lure) and practiced hour after hour in the alley behind by house. My target was a garbage can lid. It made a very nice sound when I hit it. The practice

paid off, because when I was 15 years old I came in second in the Colorado bait casting competition. Bait casting rods are short, strong, and are held with the eyes of the rod on top.

Bait casting tackle usually is used when trying to catch large, fierce fish, like bass or pike. See chapter 5 for more details.

Fly rods and reels. Fly fishing is the art and skill of fooling a fish into eating an artificial insect, minnow, or crustacean built onto a hook. All of these imitations are called "flies," and you can learn how to make them if you want to.

First of all, in fly fishing you cast the weight of the line, not the lure as in spinfishing or bait fishing. The reel, then, is mainly a holder for the line, not a part of the casting process. The rod is a very important part of fly fishing, as it pushes the line through the air to make the cast. Fly rods come in different lengths and weights, and are made of bamboo, glass fibers, boron, graphite, or mixtures of some of these. Because the rod has to push the line through the air, it must be strong, yet light in weight so your arm doesn't get too tired.

Fly rods (fig. 3-7) are made of strong, springy materials that snap back after being bent. When a heavy fly line is cast with a fly rod, it is first pulled back overhead and behind the fisherman. Then, when the line is pushed forward again the action of the rod helps push the line forward, toward the fish in the water. A really long cast can be made by someone who knows how to handle a fly rod correctly.

Fly reels are of two basic types: single-action (fig. 3-8) and automatic (fig. 3-9). Most fly fishermen prefer the single-action kind. They come in different sizes and weights and are made of different kinds of materials. The

Figure 3-7. A fly rod

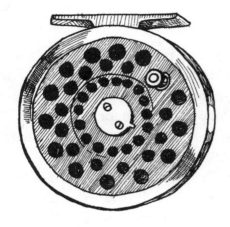

Figure 3-8. A single-action fly reel   Figure 3-9. An automatic fly reel

single-action reel has three main parts. The base, that attaches to the rod at its reel seat near the handle or grip; the spool, around which the line is wound; and the frame that holds the spool. There is a handle on the outside, attached to the spool, that is used to wind in the line. A fly reel, with its line, should weigh just enough to balance the rod when you hold it by the handle. Fly reels have a built-in drag in the form of a "click," or clutch. When it is adjusted properly, the drag makes it harder for a fish to pull line off the spool but still keeps the line from breaking. Reels are "right-handed" or "left-handed." If you are right-handed, you cast with the right hand and crank the reel with the left hand. The opposite is true if you are left-handed. Always wind the reel forward. If you have to wind it backwards you have the wrong-handed reel.

Automatic reels have a strong spring inside them. When you pull line off the reel it tightens

the spring. Then, when you push down on a lever the spring loosens, causing the line to be pulled in. There are several problems with this kind of reel. First, you cannot make long casts because the spring gets too tight to let a lot of line off the spool. Most automatic reels have a way to release the pressure but this is a bother, and besides, then there isn't enough spring power to pull in all the line that is out. Second, if you hook a really big fish and it swiftly swims away, the spring gets so tight that the line is likely to break.

Accessory equipment. Most fishermen have a tackle box (fig. 3-10) to hold their small lures, hooks, reels, and other equipment. Tackle boxes usually have compartments in them to hold different-sized objects.

There are thousands of kinds of lures, flies, and accessories, so we will mention only a few here. Sinkers (Fig. 3-11) are lead weights that carry your bait toward the bottom of the

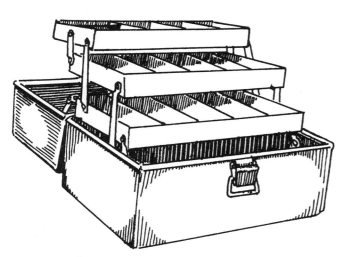

Figure 3-10. A typical tackle box. There are many other kinds.

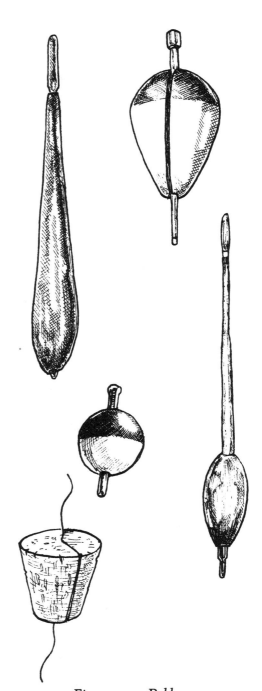

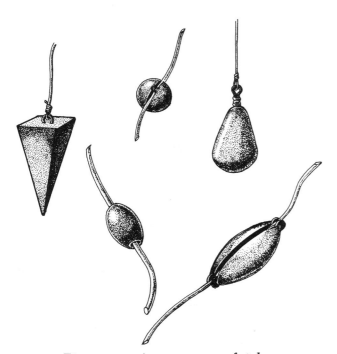

Figure 3-11. An assortment of sinkers

Figure 3-12. Bobbers

stream or lake. A bobber (fig. 3-12) is a floating device attached to the line to keep the hook off the bottom, and to let you know when a fish bites your bait. I'll tell you how to use it in chapter 4. Many fishermen use a landing net (fig. 3-13) when the fish is brought within reach. The net may have a long handle if it is used from a boat or pier, or a short handle if

it is used while wading or fishing from shore. Other small items may be in your tackle box, such as spools of leader material, fly boxes, swivels, a hook sharpener, a stringer, and a cleaning knife. Many fishermen prefer to wear a fishing vest with many pockets to hold items they may use while fishing along a river or the shores of a lake.

FIgure 3-14. Hip boots

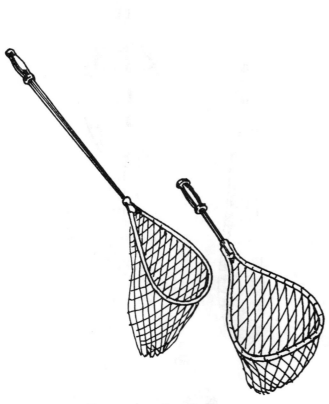

Figure 3-13. Landing nets

Wading boots. It is often necessary to use wading boots, or waders, when fishing cold lakes or rivers. Otherwise, old sneakers will do nicely. Hip boots (fig. 3-14) reach the top of the leg and are held up by attaching them to your belt. Chest waders (fig. 3-15) reach the top of your chest and are held up with suspenders. You must always be very, very careful when wading, as you can easily be swept away by fast water, or step into a deep hole, or even get stuck in deep mud. Beginning fishermen of all ages should never wade while they are alone. It is too dangerous!

Other kinds of accessories will be discussed in the chapters on kinds of fishing. But remember, no one has to have all of this equipment to catch fish. People all over the world have fun with a hook and a line tied to the end of a long stick. And they catch fish, too!

Figure 3-15. Chest waders

4. Bait Fishing

Most people begin their fishing adventures by bait fishing. The bait usually is a worm, minnow, or other live animal, but can be preserved, like salmon eggs. We must remember that bait fishing is entirely different from bait casting, even though they sound the same. Remember, bait casting uses a special kind of reel and rod to cast heavy lures, like spoons and plugs. I will discuss bait casting further in chapter 5.

Actually, nearly any kind of tackle can be used for bait fishing, because the whole idea is simply to throw the bait to where you think the fish is. These days most people use spinning tackle, but hand lines, fly rods, and even bait casting equipment can be used.

If you are fishing for bottom-feeders, like carp, suckers, and catfish, or sometimes even trout, perch, or sunfish, your bait will lay on the bottom of the lake or pond. But if the fish you wish to catch usually feeds somewhere between the bottom and the surface, you can suspend your bait off the bottom by using some kind of bobber attached to the line. This has the added advantage of telling you when a fish takes your bait, as the bobber will jiggle in the

water, begin to be pulled away, or even pulled under. That is when you jerk back to set the hook!

Bait fishing sounds simple but certain basic skills must be learned before you have much chance of catching fish. First, let's talk about baiting the hook.

Most fishermen use worms for bait. Worms are easily dug out of the ground with a shovel, but they are not found everywhere. The ground cannot be too dry or hard, and must have things in it for worms to eat, such as rotting leaves and roots. Nightcrawlers are very big worms that are found in many lawns. They come out of their burrows after dark to feed on dead leaves and to mate. If you quietly search for them with a flashlight you probably can find many, especially soon after a rain or after the lawn has been watered. But once you have spotted one, you cannot leave your light directly on it, because even though they don't have eyes they can tell when a light is shining on them. Then they vanish back down their burrows before you can catch them. When you do grab one, don't just yank it out, because it will break in half. And even if it doesn't break,

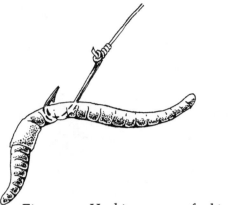

Figure 4-1. Hooking a worm for big fish

Figure 4-2. Hooking a worm for small fish

if you pull too hard its insides will burst and the worm will die in a day or two. Just pull steadily and slowly and the worm will get tired and come out. That's the way robins do it!

One more thing to remember: big worms make little worms, and when they are doing this you will find two of them tightly stuck together on the surface of the ground. It is considered very unsportsmanlike to catch them then, so leave them alone and you will have more worms to catch next year.

Now, back to baiting the hook. How you put a worm on a hook depends a lot on what kind of fish you are after. Fish with big mouths, like trout or bass, are attracted to a worm that is hooked through only once or twice (fig. 4-1). They can eat the whole worm in a single bite,

so that is the way to fish for them. But fish with smaller mouths, like sunfish or even bullhead catfish, would likely grab just the end of the worm and pull it off of the hook. So, for these fish you should put the hook through the worm in several places so the fish has to take in the hook with the worm (fig. 4-2). Of course, you would not use a five-inch night-crawler to catch a five-inch sunfish, so you might have to cut the worm into pieces and use one piece at a time.

When you use minnows for bait, it is best to hook the minnow in a place that won't kill it right away, because most fish like to eat live minnows. If you are using a bobber, it is best

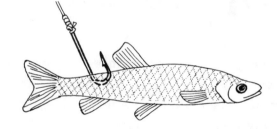

Figure 4-3. Hooking a minnow for bobber fishing

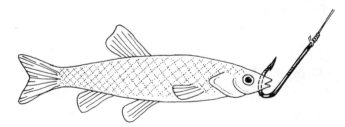

Figure 4-4. Hooking a minnow for trolling

to hook the minnow just behind the dorsal fin, close to the top so vital organs are not cut, thereby killing the bait (fig. 4-3). But if you are trolling (pulling the bait behind a boat), hook it through the lips (fig. 4-4). This will not kill it, and it will look like it is swimming naturally.

Minnows can be bought in a bait shop, or caught in a net if you know where they can be found. It is best to keep them in a minnow

Figure 4-5. A minnow bucket

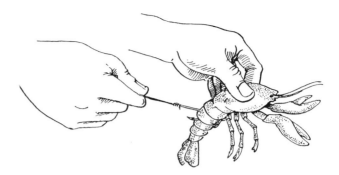

Figure 4-6. How to hold and hook a crawdad

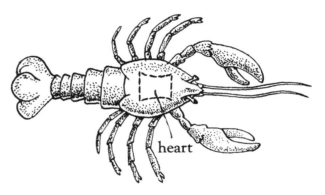

Figure 4-7. A crawdad, showing the location of the heart

bucket (fig. 4-5) so that when you want one you only have to lift the inner bucket out and then grab one. If you have to drive a long way, especially on a hot day, you probably should have an air pump to provide fresh air for them so they don't die. Inexpensive pumps can be bought that plug into a car's cigarette lighter.

About the only crustacean that is big enough for freshwater fishermen to use as bait is the crawdad (see fig. 2-14). These are easily found under rocks in almost any unpolluted water, and fish that are big enough to eat them just love them! Be careful when you handle the big ones, because they can pinch pretty hard! If you hold a crawdad by the carapace (fig. 4-6), he can't reach you.

Crawdads need fresh air just like minnows, so be sure to use an air pump. When using a crawdad for bait, don't hook it under the carapace because that is where its heart is (see fig. 4-7) and it will die at once. Instead, hook it through the abdomen (see fig. 4-6). The abdomen is usually called the "tail," although incorrectly. For example, the shrimp "tails" you eat in a restaurant are actually abdomens. Be sure to use a hook big enough so there is plenty of point to stab the fish. And if you catch no fish, the crawdads are delicious for you to eat!

Many trout and salmon fishermen use preserved salmon eggs for bait. For some reason, trout and salmon like to eat each others' eggs, so they are good bait. Preserved salmon eggs can be bought in most sporting goods stores. Fresh eggs from fish you have already caught are illegal in most states, however. One or two salmon eggs on a hook are usually enough. When you are fishing in a river, a single egg usually works best. I have found that red eggs are best for lake fishing, while yellow ones are best for rivers. I don't know why.

Other kinds of bait are used by some fishermen. Common ones are Velveeta cheese and tiny marshmallows for rainbow trout, (brown trout won't touch this kind of bait) leeches and salamander tadpoles for bass, and spleen or meat for catfish and even trout.

Now that we have described the kinds of bait, where to find it, and how to bait the hook, let's look at how to use it. There are three basic kinds of bait fishing: tightline fishing, bobber fishing, and trolling.

Tightline fishing. In tightline fishing, a weight or sinker holds the bait on the bottom of the lake (see chapter 11). The fisherman carefully reels in extra line so that the line is straight between the sinker and the tip of the rod (or the hand, if you are handline fishing). When the fish bites, the tip of the rod twitches and you know you have a bite! Jerk the rod back quickly, but not so hard as to break your rod or tear the fish's mouth.

One problem with bait fishing is that the fish might swallow the bait clear down into its

stomach, or get the hook stuck into its gills. In these cases, if you want to keep the fish, kill it before you try to tear the hook out. The best way to kill a fish is to hit it hard on the head at least three times with a stick or a rock. If the hook is in the gills, the fish will die no matter what you do, so kill it and get your hook out. But if the hook is in the stomach, and you want to release the fish (see chapter 8), simply cut the line near the fish's mouth and it probably will live for a long time back in its water. A hook doesn't cost very much and certainly is a small price to pay to keep a fish alive.

When tightline fishing it is best to put the sinker at the end of the line, with the snelled hook above it (see chapter 11). That way, the fish doesn't have to pull the weight of the sinker before you feel the bite. This type of fishing is used for most bottom-feeding fishes.

Bobber fishing. Fishing with a bobber is a great deal of fun. Honestly, I don't know of anything to compare with the thrill of seeing your bobber suddenly start to jiggle, swim off, or be pulled under, because when this happens, you know there is a fish with your hook in its mouth. There are many kinds of bobbers that can be bought in stores. Probably the most popular is the round, plastic, red and white bobber with a hook you can push out to attach to the line (fig. 3-12). These are OK, but they are not as sensitive to light nibbles from small fish as are other kinds of bobbers. Also, the line usually will slip through the bobber's hook, changing how deep your bait is. You can wrap the line around the bobber's hook several times to prevent this, but this will weaken your line in case you are lucky enough to hook a large fish. The most delicate bobber is one that is long and slender (fig. 3-12).

I have had great success using a simple stick tied at each of its ends to the line (fig. 4-8). When a fish bites, the stick will go down at one end, and up at the other, a sure sign that a fish is attacking the bait. Learning to know when a fish is just nibbling at the bait, and when it is seriously trying to eat it is a skill that can be learned only by experience.

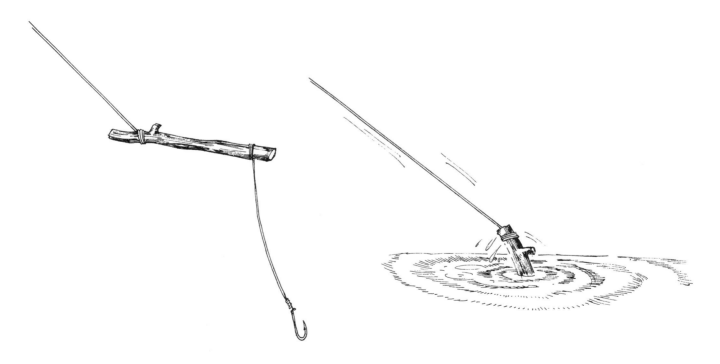

Figure 4-8. Using a stick for a bobber

Trolling. Pulling the bait or lure behind a boat is a very popular way to fish for those who can afford to own or rent a boat. You may be able to catch many fish this way if you use the right bait or lure. Simply let your line out for a distance and hold your rod, hoping for a bite. How far you let your line out depends on many things. The longer the line is out, the deeper your bait will be. The speed at which you are trolling also will affect the depth of your bait: if you troll fast it will come closer to the surface; if you troll slower your bait will go deeper. So, some practice at trolling is needed to get it right. You can troll from a large power boat, a small rowboat, or even a tiny rubber raft. I have had a lot of fun fishing from a rubber raft, with both hands on the oars and a fishing rod stuck between my knees! When a fish bites it is exciting to drop the oars, grab the rod, and set the hook as fast as possible. Usually the fish will hook itself.

When you are bait fishing, any kind of bait that you think will work probably will. Use your imagination. I once saw a boy catch a seventeen-inch rainbow trout using a piece of raw bacon for bait! Most experienced fishermen would have said it couldn't be done.

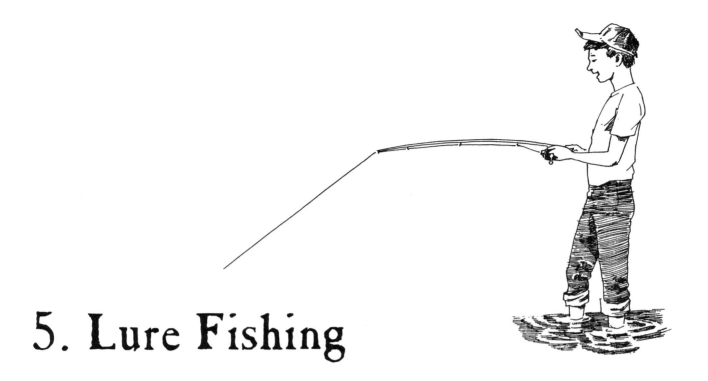

5. Lure Fishing

Lures are not made of real animals, but they may look a lot like them. Some look very much like minnows or crayfish, for example, but are made of plastic or rubber. Two main kinds of lures are those that imitate live, real animals, and those that somehow attract a fish to bite even though they don't look like anything real.

Fly fishing really falls into this kind of fishing, but because different kinds of equipment are needed, I have written a about the use of flies in chapter 6.

For many years lure fishing was done mostly with a bait casting rod and reel (see fig. 3-1). Today, many people use spinning tackle for lure fishing as it is much easier, and lures of lighter weight can be cast. Most lures are rather heavy and it is their weight that you cast. Bait casting reels are difficult to use and need a lot of practice before you can use them well, while spinning tackle is rather easy.

Thousands of kinds of lures have been invented. Each fisherman seems to have a favorite. One basic type is the plug (fig. 5-1), a heavy lure that tricks fish into thinking it is a living thing meant to be eaten by hungry fish. Plugs may splash across the surface of the water, or dive down beneath the surface. Some look like small fish or other favorite fish foods, while others are pretty strange looking, but catch fish anyway.

Spinners. An excellent lure, especially for use with light-weight tackle is the spinner (fig. 5-2). Spinners are made of a piece of wire with a round or oval blade loosely attached to it, followed by a hook. When the spinner is pulled through the water the blade spins around the wire, shining and sparkling as it goes. Fish may get very excited about the sparkling blade and often will bite on the spinner and get themselves hooked. I have found that the slower you pull the spinner through the water, while still keeping the blade spinning, the more likely it is that you will get a strike. Spinners work well in both lakes and streams.

Spoons. Still another kind of basic lure is the spoon, or wobbler (fig. 5-3). Spoons look a bit like a table spoon without a handle and with a hook at the back end. When pulled slowly through the water, they wobble from side to

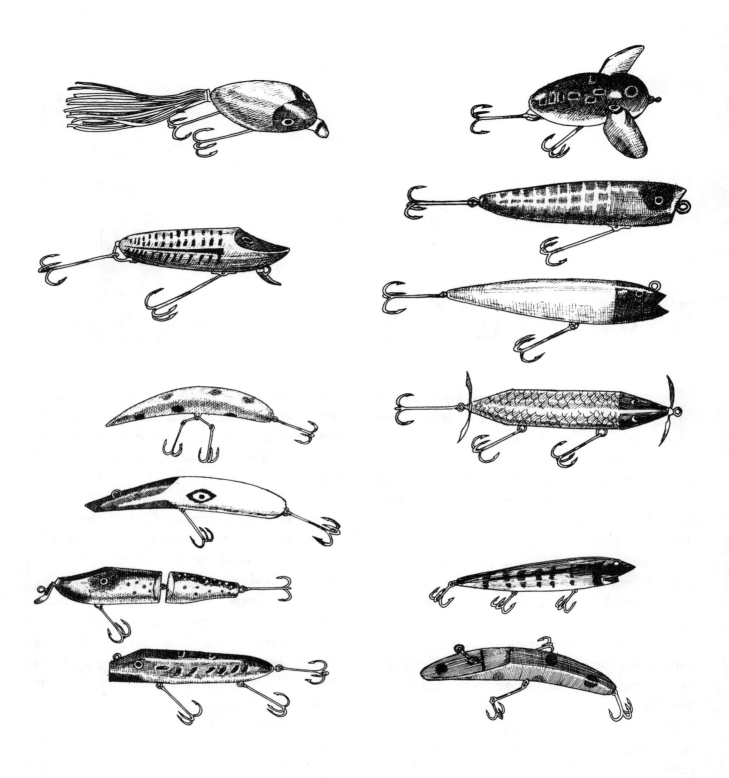

Figure 5-1. *Several types of surface and diving plugs*

side instead of spinning. If they are pulled too fast they will spin and twist up your line. Spoons can be used with any kind of fishing tackle, but the tiny ones with little weight are best used with spinning rods and reels. Spoons are very deadly on all kinds of gamefish that have mouths large enough to try to eat them.

Jigs. There are many other kinds of lures that you can use. Artificial worms, minnows, and crayfish can be bought, as can jigs (fig 5-4). Jigs have a heavy, metal head followed by feathers, fur, rubber strips, or other fish attractors. They are cast out, allowed to sink to near the bottom, then are reeled back, using short jerks of the rod to make them look alive. They may look silly, but they do work well.

Figure 5-3. Spoons

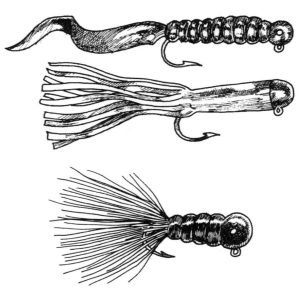

Figure 5-4. Jigs

Figure 5-2. Spinners

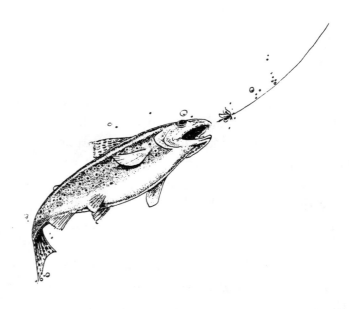

6. Fly Fishing

Fly fishing is more challenging than other types of fishing for me, because you must trick the fish into thinking that your fly is an actual, living animal. Casting these flies is fun in itself, too. Fly fishing is a name used for fishing with a lure made of feathers, fur, hair, and other materials. Most importantly, this kind of fishing uses a special fly rod, and fly reel, and uses the weight of the line to cast the fly, rather than the weight of the fly itself. This kind of tackle is described in chapter 3.

Flies imitate insects that live in and out of the water, as well as other creatures such as crustaceans and small fishes. The flies that we use are of different types and require different techniques to fish with them: Dry flies (fig. 6-1) float on the surface of the water. Wet flies (fig. 6-2) are meant to sink when used. Nymphs (fig. 6-3) also sink, but look like larval or pupal stages of insects. Streamers (fig. 6-4) are meant to look like small fish swimming. Let's look at each type of fly and how to use it.

Dry flies. Floating, dry flies are mostly used to catch trout, but many sunfish (including bass) and other fish occasionally will bite on them. Fish that normally feed on the bottom of lakes and streams, such as catfish, carp, and suckers, are not usually interested in what floats on the surface of their world, although I have caught them now and then on dry flies. Also, large fish eaters like pike, muskies, and even perch are not interested in delicate, floating flies. The kinds of insects that fish eat are discussed in chapter 2.

A dry fly is made to be very lightweight so that it floats easily. Many kinds of dry fly oils can be bought that will help the fly float longer. These are pastes or liquids that are smeared on the fly to make it waterproof. It has to be smeared on again after a few casts to work, though, and after a fish is caught the fly must be washed in the stream or lake to remove the fish's slime. Then the fly should be pressed between folds of cloth (usually my shirt!), fluffed up again by blowing on it, and covered with more dry fly oil. This may sound like a lot of bothersome work, but the thrill of watching a fish swim to the surface of the water and suck in your fly is surely worth the effort.

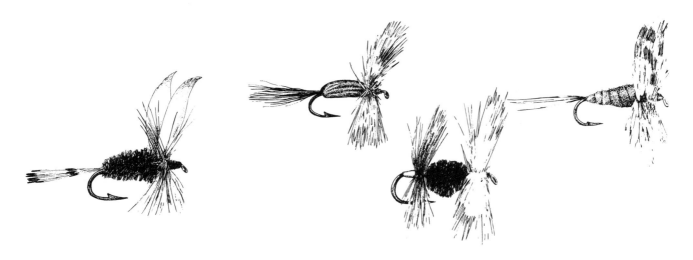

Figure 6-1. *Several patterns of dry flies*

Figure 6-2. *Some kinds of wet flies*

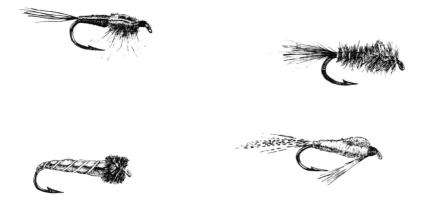

Figure 6-3. *Nymph imitations*

Figure 6-4. Some patterns of streamers

While fishing with a dry fly, there are some difficulties involved. For example, while we want our fly to float, we also want our leader to sink. Leaders (see chapter 3) have a very strong desire to float. When they do, they bend the surface of the water, make shadows, and otherwise make the fish think that all is not natural up there, so then they won't bite. A lot of things affect the visibility of the leader, such as how fast and ripply the water in a river is, how many ripples (tiny waves) there are on the surface of a wind-blown lake, or how dark it is. Several brands of "leader sink" can be bought, but they wash off the leader after only a few casts. Saliva from your mouth, or mud also are good leader sinks for a few casts. Sinking the leader is one of the fly fisherman's greatest frustrations.

Fly leaders usually are tapered, which means they are thickest at the base, where they join with the line, then become thinner toward the fly itself. How thin it becomes is the choice of the fisherman, who decides how big and strong the fish might be and how easily the fish might

be scared by a thick leader. The thin end of the leader is called the tippet. I will show you how to tie on a tippet in chapter 11.

The fly line also is available in different kinds. First of all, they are made in different shapes. For example, some lines are level, or of equal size throughout their length, while a tapered line is thick at its base and thin at its tip. A double tapered line is thickest in the middle, becoming thinner at each end. Really, that makes it two lines, because as one end wears out you can change it around and have a brand-new line. A very popular line today is the weight forward line, which has most of its weight near one end, followed by a rapidly tapered end. You can cast this line a little farther.

Another variation in fly lines is the weight of the line. For dry fly fishing we use a floating line, which is easy to lift off of the water and won't sink, carrying the fly down with it. For wet flies, nymphs, and streamers, a sinking line is best because it does help sink the fly to where the fish might be waiting. Then there is a sinking tip line for those times when you want the

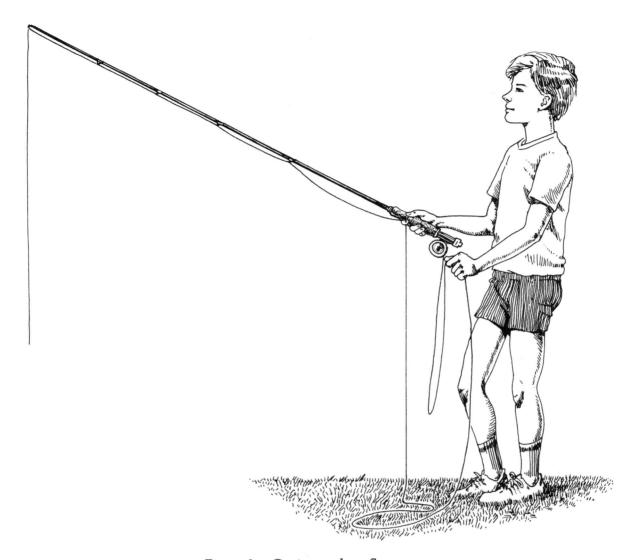

Figure 6-5. Getting ready to fly cast

fly to sink but most of the line to float. This kind of line is most useful when fishing with nymph imitations. The process sometimes works better if you wrap a bit of lead around the end of the line. This kind of "sinker" can be bought in tackle shops.

Fly casting is entirely different from any other kind of casting. You can practice on your lawn or any other flat place until you get the hang of it. It's really not very hard to do, after you understand a few things about it. Practice at first with no leader or fly attached to the line, but rather tie a tiny bright ribbon in a knot at the end of the line so you can see it.

First, thread the line through the guides (or eyes) of the rod. Make sure you do not miss any, and that you do not wrap the line around the rod. Next, pull a few feet of line off the reel and let it pile up in front of your feet (fig. 6-5). You don't need a lot of line at first, because the farther you try to cast the more problems you will have. Besides, casting a short line teaches you how to cast a long one.

Hold the rod handle in a comfortable way (fig. 6-6) and hold on to the line lightly with the other hand. Cast the rod forward and you will see that the line flies over your head and lands straight out in front of you (fig. 6-7). Try

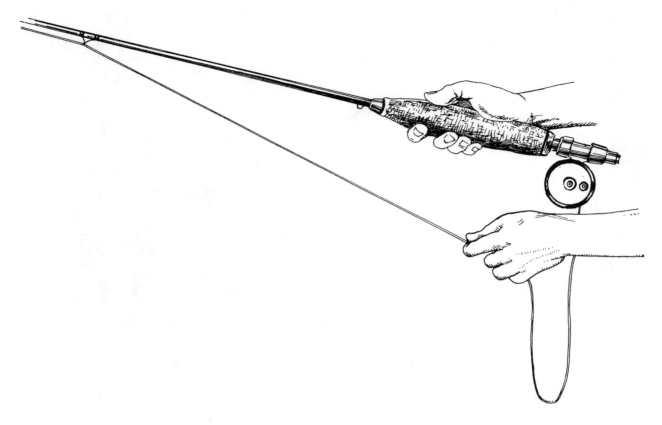

Figure 6-6. Proper way to hold the rod and line when fly casting

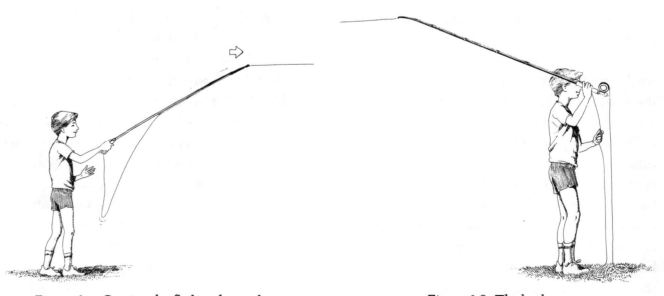

Figure 6-7. Casting the fly line forward

Figure 6-8. The back cast

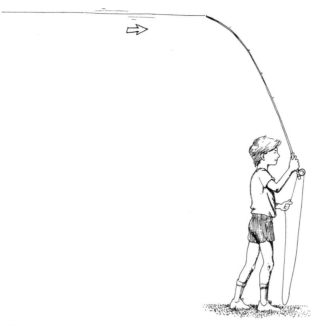

Figure 6-9. *Beginning the forward cast*

this a few times with 10 or 15 feet of line out, but holding onto the line so that the extra loose line at your feet does not move up into the rod's guides. Lift the line off the ground with a single strong but steady pull. It should fly over your head and hang straight out from the tip of your rod behind you (fig. 6-8). Before it can fall to the ground, cast it forward again (fig. 6-9). Figure 6-10 shows the whole process in action. With a little practice you will have mastered the basic skill of fly casting.

Of course, something always can go wrong. If you cast forward before the line has straightened out behind you, it will snap like a whip. When you hear this you know your timing is off. Besides, if a fly were attached to your leader and you did this, the fly would snap off and you would never see it again.

Figure 6-10. *The different steps in fly casting*

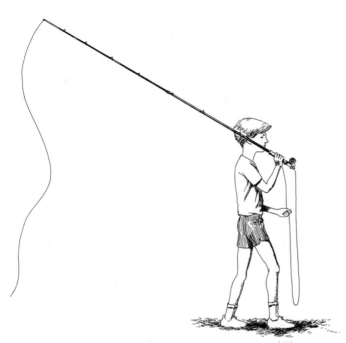

Figure 6-11. If you wait too long, your line will fall to the ground behind you and hook a bush, or rock, or . . .

But if you wait too long on the back cast, the fly would hit the ground, or rock, or bush, and break off when you try to cast forward again (fig. 6-11). Also, when the fly is too low it might hit you on the head. I can tell you from experience that a fishhook in the ear or neck is very painful!

Now, to make a longer cast, wait until the line shoots in front of you and then let go of the line that lies on the ground, letting it run loosely through your fingers. Grab it again after a few feet of line have gone out and it should straighten out and fall to the surface. It is best to stop the line so it is straight and about a foot above the water. That way, when it comes down it won't make a big splash. It also is possible to increase the length of the line being cast by releasing extra line on the back cast, but this takes a bit more practice. And remember to look out for trees, bushes, and other things on your back cast. I once hooked an automobile passing by behind me—it was great sport for an instant but my leader was not strong enough to hold it, so it got away!

Now that you know how to cast a fly, let's see how it is done to catch fish. As I said earlier,

Figure 6-12. . . . smack you on the back of the head when you try to cast forward!

dry flies are meant to float on the surface of the water. In some ways this is an easy way to fish, because you actually can see the fish eat the fly. But in other ways it is harder, because the floating line is pulled around by the currents of a river or ripples of a lake. Currents make the fly "drag" across the surface in a way no living insect would float (fig. 6-13). Fish notice this and usually will not take such a fly. So the really hard part of dry fly fishing is being able to lay your line on the water so that loose line will be pulled away first by any faster water between you and where you think the fish might be (fig. 6-14). This technique gives the fly a few seconds to float naturally, which may be all the time the fish needs to swim to the surface and grab it.

The roll cast may be useful, especially if there is a bank or bushes right behind you. Its really not hard to do but takes a bit of practice. Lift the rod tip until it is about straight up while pulling in the line. When just a few feet of the

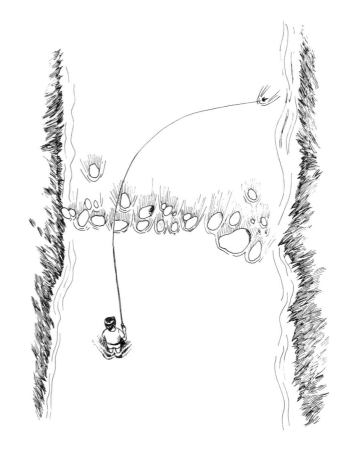

Figure 6-13. A fly dragging across current

Figure 6-14. The line landing on the water in curves to prevent drag for a few seconds

line extend before you, make a forward cast before you lift the line off the water. The line will roll away from you to land straight out. This is best for short casts, but when you are good at it, you can place your fly quite a distance out.

Always remember that fish can see very well, especially in clear, shallow water, so sneak up on them from behind, bending down if you have to. And while fish do not seem to pay attention to people talking, they can hear your footsteps very well, so walk quietly.

Knowing what kind of fly to use is a science in itself, but a bit of common sense will help. If there is a big hatch of mayflies, use a fly about the same size and shape as the live insects. Colors are not as important. If stoneflies are emerging, use a stonefly imitation, and so on.

If there is no particular hatch going on, any fly may work. In any case, use the thinnest tippet you think won't break too easily, for, as I have said, fish have very good eyesight.

Wet flies. There are many kinds of wet flies (fig. 6-2) that can be used. Usually they work best in ponds and lakes where fish are not as used to feeding on the surface, but this certainly is not always true. Wet flies are meant to sink as fast as possible, so usually they are used with a sinking line.

When you think you know where a fish might be in a river, cast ahead of it so the fly sinks by the time it is swept down to the fish (fig. 6-15). It is harder to know when a fish takes a wet fly than a dry fly because usually you cannot see the fly itself. It is best to watch the line, and the second it stops or even slows down, give a sharp jerk to set the hook. Most times something other than a fish has caused

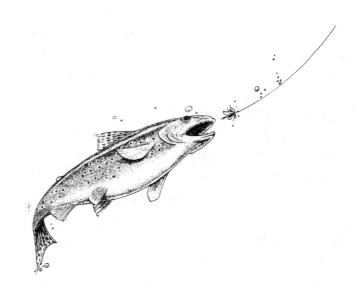

Figure 6-15. A fly drifting downstream toward a trout

this, so you hook nothing but a stick or rock, but many fish are caught this way.

Wet fly fishing in a lake or pond is much easier than in a river. When you get to a place where you think fish might be, cast onto the water and let the fly and line sink almost to the bottom. Then pull the line back slowly, either steadily or in short jerks. It is easy to feel a strike so you can set the hook. I have caught dozens of sunfish and even trout this way in a single day or evening.

If you are in a boat of any kind, moving very slowly, you can let out a lot of line and troll with a wet fly, nymph, or streamer—a method called harling (fig. 6-16). This can be very rewarding for the fisherman and takes very little effort.

Nymphs. Fishing with nymphs is just like wet fly fishing, except that the fly pattern you use imitates a juvenile stage of insect or a small crustacean.

Figure 6-16. Harling

Streamers. Streamer flies (fig. 6-4) imitate small fish, a favorite food of large fish. Harling is one way to fish with them, and another is to fish them just like casting wet flies in a lake. But the real challenge is to cast streamers to trout in a river. Very big fish often are caught this way.

A basic difference in casting streamers in a river is that usually you fish downstream instead of upstream. After you decide where a fish might be, let the fly sink down in front of it on a tight line. That is, the streamer should move as if it were a small fish struggling against the current. This can be done by two basic methods: Stand in shallow water above a deep pool (but be very careful not to be swept away by the current) and let enough line out to reach deep into the pool (fig. 6-17). Then pull it back with short jerks. When a fish hits that fly you'll know it! Or, you can cast across the stream, then let lots of line out so the fly sinks. Let the current pull the fly downstream (fig. 6-18). You will get most strikes while the fly is drifting downstream. When the fly is straight below you, slowly pull it back toward you. Streamer fly fishing takes lots of practice, but it can be very good fun and always gives you the chance of catching a big one.

Any of these flies can be used with success when fished behind a spinning "bubble" (fig. 11-14). Used with a spinning rod and reel, the bubble, which can be filled partly or fully with water for added weight, is rigged with a few feet of line or leader material behind it. With a fly on the end, it can be cast a long distance into a lake or river, to be slowly pulled in (trolled) in hopes of attracting a strike. This is a highly successful method, especially fishing for trout in lakes.

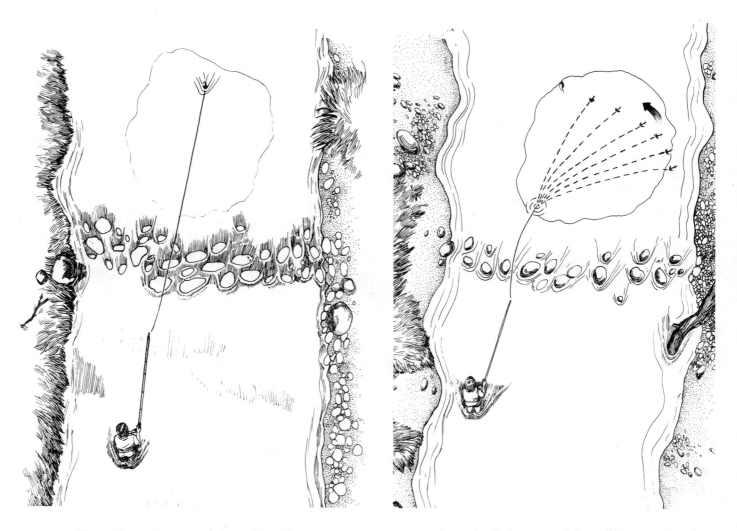

Figure 6-17. Streamer fishing downstream

Figure 6-18. Streamer fishing across stream

It is interesting and fun to tie your own flies instead of buying them, and even a very young person can learn how to do it, especially with a teacher or guide book. I hope you will try it someday.

7. Ice Fishing

Ice fishing usually is done in lakes. It is quite safe when the ice is thick and hard, but very dangerous when it is thin or soft. So, if you plan to enjoy this sport, be sure the ice is in proper condition. And remember that at the end of winter the ice may still be thick, but it becomes mushy and dangerous to walk on.

Another important thing to think about before you even leave home to go fishing is that you will need very warm clothing. Winter weather can be deadly to the fisherman who is not dressed for it. It always is best to go with someone who has experience and who can help you decide what to wear and what kind of tackle you will need. Never ice fish by yourself, because if you fall through the ice, no one will know.

Obviously, you can't fish without a hole in the ice. Several kinds of tools are made to help you cut such a hole. The simplest is called a **spud** (fig. 7-1). This is a heavy bar with a sharp, flat end. You chip away at the ice until you make a hole. The bottom edge of the ice will be rough and can cut your line, so smooth it with the spud. Be careful that you do not drop it through the hole! The hole does not need to be very wide, just eight inches or so. Some states have a law against making a large hole, because someone could step into it!

Another hole driller is the **auger**. There are two types of augers. The spoon auger (fig. 7-2) has a razor-sharp edge that shaves ice away when you push down and turn the handle. The screw auger (fig. 7-3) bores through the ice like a large drill. Some even come equipped with a gas-powered engine!

After the hole is bored, you will need a strainer to dip out the ice shavings. You can buy one specially made for this at a tackle shop (fig. 7-4), but a kitchen tea strainer also works very well.

How you fish through the ice depends on the kind of fish you are trying to catch. You can use live bait, dead bait, flies, or lures, depending on the situation. The same can be said for the kinds of tackle used.

Many people use their spinning rod and reel and simply drop their baited hook, with a sinker on the line, down the hole until it hits bottom, then reel it up a foot or two. Fishing this way, you can either hold the rod until you

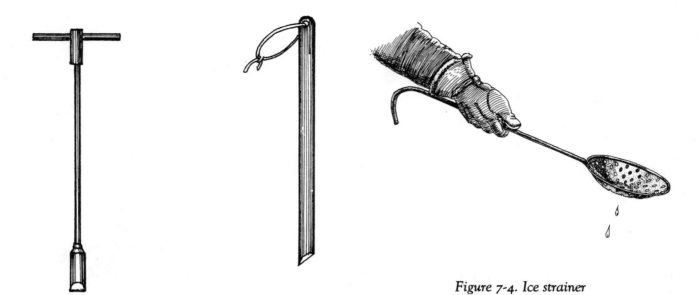

Figure 7-1. An ice spud

Figure 7-4. Ice strainer

Figure 7-2. Spoon auger

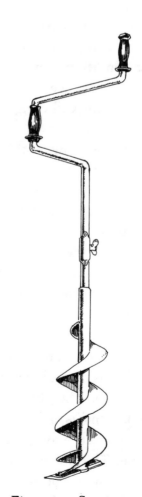

Figure 7-3. Screw auger

Figure 7-5. Using an ice fishing rod

feel the bite, or set the rod down and watch for the tip end to jiggle. A slightly different way is to attach a small bobber to the line and watch until a fish pulls it down. A problem here is that if you are back by the rod handle and reel, you can't see the bobber. So I like to use an **ice fishing rod** (fig. 7-5), which is short enough to be able to sit next to the hole. When the bobber goes down, jerk up with the rod. If you hook a fish you either can reel it up or grab the line, drop the rod, and pull the line up by hand. When the fish gets to the bottom of the hole, be careful—the hook or even the fish itself may get caught on the edge of the ice and pull off. Once the fish's head is in the hole, it is easy to slide it out. And when it's lying on the ice, you won't have to worry about it spoiling in the sun!

What kinds of bait should you use? Well, that depends on the kind of fish you want to catch. First of all, some fish, like catfish, don't often bite in the winter, so it is not much use to try for them. Many fish like live minnows. Fish such as crappie, perch, pike, bass, walleye,

and trout really go for them. Usually you can buy live minnows at a bait shop during the winter. Bluegills and other sunfish bite fast at insect larvae such as "mousies" (a kind of fly) and "waxworms" (a kind of moth). You can buy these at many bait shops or order them by mail from suppliers listed in the back of fishing magazines. Preserved salmon eggs (available in tackle shops) are excellent bait for trout, especially rainbows, and Velveeta cheese also works well for rainbow trout. Earthworms are good for most kinds of fish, even the brown trout, which is pretty picky about what it eats, especially in the winter. Actually, whatever a fish eats in the summer it will eat in the winter.

If you want to use artificial lures, that can be done too. I have had great success catching trout with weighted flies, such as a "hare's ear" (fig. 7-3) or a tiny weighted jig. Perch and other fishes will bite on these too. Just slowly jiggle them up and down. You will easily feel a fish if it strikes.

Still another kind of tackle used in some parts of America is the **tip-up** (fig. 7-6). It is

Figure 7-6. A tip-up in action

not legal in all states. Usually it is used to catch large, predatory fish, like pike, pickerel, walleye, and bass. Simply, it is a spring with a line attached to it, with a hook and bait. When a fish bites and pulls a bit of line out, the spring releases, the hook is jerked, and a flag comes up to let the fisherman know he has a fish. Many tip-ups can be used at a time.

Except on sunny, quiet days, ice fishing is hard work. Drilling holes to find fish, keeping the hole free of blowing snow and freezing ice, and preventing your equipment from blowing away is a lot of work. In some northern states, people build little houses (ice shanties) that they pull over the hole in the ice. They can sit in their shanty with a warm heater and be very comfortable. But if you have to keep digging new holes to find out where the fish are, this is not a good idea. Besides, in most western states the wind blows so hard that your shanty might be tipped over or slide across the lake. It has been said that ice shanties have been found halfway up mountainsides in the following summer, but I don't think I believe it. At any rate, ice fishing is a challenging way to fish if you can't wait until summer.

8. Catch and Release

These days there are so many fishermen and so few fish that it is not wise to kill all the fish you catch. If a fish is released without a great deal of harm, it will continue to live and grow to give other fishermen the pleasure of catching it later. In fact, in some streams, every big fish has been caught and released many times.

Most states have a daily limit on how many fish you may keep, and a total possession limit as well. These laws must be strictly upheld by the fisherman. But just because the daily limit is six, for example, doesn't mean you have to kill that many. Usually I keep just one or a few, depending on the species of fish, then release any others I may catch. Often you will catch a fish that is too small to keep anyway. Of course, if a fish is hooked in the gills and is bleeding, it probably will die if you release it. Such a fish should be kept no matter what its size, unless it is smaller than the legal size limit. Some fishermen use hooks without barbs so the hook is easily removed. All you need to do to fish with a barbless hook is simply bend the barb down with a pair of pliers.

In many streams and lakes the law allows catch and release only, so you are not allowed to kill any fish. In such places bait is not allowed, as a fish is much more likely to swallow bait than a fly or lure. But even if it does swallow the hook, it usually will live if you cut your snell or line at about the level of the fish's jaw (fig. 8-1). A hook does not cost much, and it surely is a small price to pay to save the life of such a beautiful animal.

A fish is easily harmed, especially when out of the water, so you must know how to handle it and release it properly. First of all, if you think you will release it, don't yank it out of the water to flop around in the rocks or dirt. Instead, find a place where you can gently pull the fish into shallow water until it is lying on its side. Then hold it firmly but gently in one hand and take out the hook with the other. Fish are very slippery but even so, don't squeeze them hard or you will break some of their internal organs. If this happens, the fish will look and act normally when released, but it will slowly die later on.

Remember too, that some fish have sharp spines that can hurt. Catfish and perch are ex-

Figure 8-1. Cutting the leader before releasing a fish that has swallowed the hook

Figure 8-2. Reviving a fish by pushing water over its gills

amples, so be careful. Walleye and pike have big, sharp teeth, so be careful of these, too.

When you release a fish, especially a delicate species like a trout, turn it right side up in the water and slowly push and pull it through the water, or hold it so it faces down stream, so that water will flow over its gills (fig. 8-2). Usually it will recover and swim away very quickly. Maybe you will catch the same fish again someday when it is much larger!

So remember, killing as many fish as possible is not the mark of a good fisherman. Catching fish just the way you want to and releasing most of them shows that you care about the conservation of the fish and its habitat for both the fish and for future fishermen.

9. Reading the Water of Ponds and Lakes

When you are first learning to fish, a pond or lake looks pretty much the same all over. However, there is much variety in water, because the bottom and shoreline are different from one spot to another. For example, the water may be very deep close to shore in one place but shallow only a few feet away (fig. 9-1). One spot may have a rocky bottom while another is sandy or muddy. The kind of bottom and the depth of the water determines what kind of plants will grow there. Different plants allow different kinds of insects, crustaceans, and minnows to live in different places. Because bigger fish eat bigger prey, they will be found in special areas in the pond where the right plant for that kind of food grows.

Not only are fish found in different places, but they will change locations at different times of the year because water temperature and plant growth also change. So a knowledge of all of these facts can make the difference between catching or not catching fish. Many times I have seen fishermen fishing in the wrong spot or using the wrong tackle for that place, while wondering why other people are catching fish and they are not.

It is difficult to tell you just where to fish, because each lake is different. But a few simple ideas can help you. First, think about rocky bottoms. These are easy for bait fishermen to find because they snag their hook or sinker nearly every cast. But this kind of habitat is attractive to brown trout, walleye, and other species that like to eat crayfish and minnows (fig. 9-2). Sometimes an underwater hill or ridge extends quite far out into the lake. When you can find these while in your boat, you may discover that fish have gotten together in large numbers. If you catch one, try to remember just where it was and chances are you will catch more in the same spot.

Much can be said for weed beds. Many kinds of fish lurk around them, feeding on insects and so on, while larger fish hide in the weeds to catch smaller ones (fig. 9-3). These are places you can find pike, bass, rainbow trout, crappie, and others. To find a weed bed, just let your hook and sinker fall to the bottom. If there is a weed you will hook it! Reeds, cattails, and water lilies around the bank are favorite places for fish to feed. Casting a fly or bait with a bobber, or a lure along the edge of such a place may be very productive.

Figure 9-1. A typical pond, showing variations in the bottom

Figure 9-2. A bass attacking a crayfish

Figure 9-3. The little fish had better look out!

Figure 9-4. Bluegills guard their nests against other fish

*Figure 9-5. A beaver dam with brook trout waiting to
be caught*

Some fish dig shallow nests and lay their eggs in shallow water near the sandy bank and guard their eggs against other hungry fish (fig. 9-4). If the water is clear you may be able to see them. For example, sunfish, bass, and crappie are easily caught at such times, but don't try to catch these spawning fish because once they have been caught, other fish will surely eat their eggs. That means fewer fish for some future year.

Remember that some fish feed at night and others during the day. I have found that brown trout feed best on cloudy or stormy days, while rainbows don't seem to care much either way. These differences apply to many kinds of fish.

Brook trout usually are found where the bottom is muddy, such as in beaver ponds (fig. 9-5), while lake trout come close to shore only in the early spring just as the ice is melting off. Perch are caught anywhere from shallow shorelines to very deep lake bottoms, probably depending on where food is found at the time. Submerged trees, logs, sagebrush, and so on are always good places to find fish, although it is easy to snag your hook there.

In trout lakes, and to some extent bass lakes, adult insects hatch at certain times of the year and certain hours of the day. Then surface fishing with a fly and bubble can be terrific! Caddisflies emerge like this too, but are very difficult to imitate. Damselflies emerge only during the day, usually at midday.

Reading the surface of the lake is important, too. Fishing usually is better when small ripples or waves are present. Even fly fishing seems to improve when a small wind comes up. An exception to this is at night, when still water may be better. Cloudy conditions, even rain or snow, make fish more active and interested in feeding. Sunrise and sunset are my two favorite times to fish. But I don't much like getting up early, so I prefer the evening. I have watched many people pack up and head for home at early evening, just when the fishing will probably start to be at its best.

Ask local fishermen about the best places to fish, if you are not familiar with a pond or lake. If you can go back often, try experimenting in different parts of the lake using various kinds of flies, lures, or bait. Soon you will be the expert and people will ask for your advice!

10. Reading the Water of Streams and Rivers

Fish in streams and rivers have one thing in common with those in ponds and lakes. They are looking for food. But lake fish often have to swim around looking for their dinners, while river fish wait for the rushing water to bring food to them. This is not to say that river fish never move from place to place, because just as in lakes the animals they eat are present at different times of the day in different places.

The ideal place for a fish to live in a stream is where the current is not so strong that the fish gets tired just holding its place, but also in a location where it can easily see food passing by either on the surface or underwater. At the same time, the fish must protect itself from birds and mammals that like to eat it, by staying in water too deep to be easily seen. A good river fisherman must know these things and present the bait or lure in a way that the fish does not suspect anything unnatural.

There are so many kinds of streams and rivers that it is impossible to describe them all. A tiny trickle of water in the Rocky Mountains may have trout in it, but the mighty Mississippi River, a mile across, also has fish in it that can

be caught. So let's just look at some general principles that apply to fishing in nearly all moving water.

First, fish need to rest near the bottom in water that is not too swift to sweep them away. When you look at a piece of water, what do you see? Is it relatively slow moving, with perhaps a log or rock to break the force of the current? Or is it in turmoil, with water swirling around and up, or maybe in the opposite direction of the river's flow? Fish seldom are found in swirling water because they cannot maintain their position and cannot very well see what food tidbits are passing by.

Second, is there bright sunlight on the water where you think a fish might be? Unless the water is quite deep or muddy, no fish is likely to be there in a feeding mood. Fish have no eyelids to close off the bright light. Also, most aquatic insects do not emerge during bright light, because they will dry up before their wings and other body parts can harden to protect them.

Basically, fish live in three main parts of a river: pocket water, runs, and pools.

Figure 10-1. An underwater view of pocket water

Pocket water. Pockets of water are formed behind rocks, logs, and other objects in the stream (fig 10-1). The water rushes around and over an object, like a big rock, and suddenly becomes slow for a short time, forming a pocket. Fish, especially trout, do very well here, eating whatever goodies the water brings them. This also is the easiest place for a fisherman to catch trout, because it is easy to walk upstream toward them, and fish cannot see well behind themselves. Dry or wet flies have only to be cast ahead of where the trout is likely to be and the fly is brought to the fish as a feast from the river. But be careful that your leader and line do not splash on top of the fish, because fish can sense the line and will not bite. However, a dry fly dropped a foot or two in front of a fish catches its attention and often the fish itself. Pocket water fishing can be very productive and you usually only need a short bit of line to do it.

Runs. A run (fig. 10-2) is a fairly deep, long stretch of water that may contain fish along its entire length. These fish get most of their food from aquatic animals rather than terrestrials, but when a hatch of mayflies, for instance, happens, dozens of fish may suddenly begin feeding on or near the surface. During the night, trout may move from the deep run to shallows at the sides. I have caught big rainbows in one or two feet of water early in the morning next to a deep run. But by the time the sun hits the water they are gone to deeper places. Runs usually are deep on one side and shallow on the other, although exceptions occur.

Pools. Many pools (fig. 10-3) are not very productive except for bait fishermen who put their bait on or near the bottom. A pool is a giant pocket of water where the fish don't seem as interested in swimming around to find food. I think they use them as fish resort motels where they can rest, avoid the sun, and maybe even make friends. I have had very poor luck in catching fish in such places, with one exception: at sunset, fish, especially trout and walleye, are likely to move out of the pool to the shallow water at the head or side of the pool to catch food. Then you have a much better chance to catch them. I discussed fishing pools with streamer flies in Chapter 6.

What I have described about small streams and rivers applies also to big rivers. Because they are so wide and deep, it is more difficult to read the water. Sometimes a boat is necessary to get to where the fish are. It usually is best to learn to fish big rivers when you are with someone who is an expert and can help you.

Because the stream bottom is made up of rocks, sticks, sand, and so on, it affects the way the water surface looks. When you learn to read the surface you can guess what the bottom is like. Then you will know if fish are likely to be present and what you will have to do to catch them.

For example, if a large rock is on the bottom, the water will suddenly move much faster as it passes over it. This means that there is a deep pocket behind the rock where fish are likely to be (fig. 10-1). Remember that you always want to get your bait, lure, or fly (except dry flies) down to the fish's level by the time it reaches the fish. So in this case, let us say you are trying to catch a trout with a worm. You should have a sinker attached a few inches above the hook. Cast in front of the rock, letting your line slide past or over the rock, then have it quickly sink to the bottom. Keep your line straight and tight, lifting it up and down as you feel it hit the bottom. If there is a trout there, it probably will grab your worm. You might feel a sharp jerk on the line or it might simply stop moving downstream with the water. If you even suspect that you have a bite, give a short, sharp jerk with the rod tip. You will lose a lot of hooks to snags this way, but that is to be expected. These few simple ideas also apply to runs and pools.

Reading the surface is even more important for dry fly fishing. You want your fly to float downstream like a live insect, but between the fly and your rod tip is a length of floating line. This line is at the mercy of the currents, which can pull your fly under or make it slide across the water's surface.

The successful river fisherman is the person who learns to read the water. Understanding the water takes a lot of practice but is as much fun as actually catching fish!

Figure 10-2. A run

Figure 10-3. A pool

11. How to Tie Knots and Rigs

The weakest parts of any fishing line are its knots. When the line or leader is twisted around and tightened down, it tends to cut itself. Some knots are weaker than others so should not be used. Other knots that might be strong are so big or so hard to tie that they really are not worth using.

When we combine knots, lines, hooks, swivels, sinkers, and so on, we call the result a rig. It is absolutely necessary for the fisherman to know how to tie a few basic knots and rigs.

Knots. There are two basic ways that a hook can be attached to the line, either directly or with the use of a snell (see chapter 3). A very good knot for direct attachment is the improved clinch knot (fig. 11-1). This knot takes a little practice but soon becomes simple to tie. Even so, sometimes it will slip, so, as with all knots, pull on it hard to make sure it won't slip. But be careful not to stick your finger with the hook! Study the diagram in figure 11-1 and practice until you can do it.

You can buy snelled hooks but you can also snell them yourself much cheaper, so let's learn how to do it. Then I will describe how to attach a snelled hook to the line.

First cut a short piece of monofilament line, about ten inches long. Hold the hook upside down between your thumb and first finger. Push one end of the monofilament into the front of the hook's eye until it passes the bend of the hook (fig. 11-2a). Then hold it tightly next to the hook with the same fingers. Bend the other end of the monofilament and push it through the eye in the opposite direction, until about an inch sticks out (fig. 11-2b). Hold the line next to the shank of the hook between your thumb and first finger, next to the one you already are holding. Now comes the tricky part. In the diagram, you can see that you have formed a big, round loop of line. Hold this loop with your other hand close to the eye of the hook and wrap it around the front end of the hook from just behind the eye toward the bend (fig. 11-2c). Wrap about five tight turns, always keeping the rest of the line tightly between your fingers. Then pull the end sticking out of the eye forward until the loop is gone (fig. 11-2d). I usually use my teeth for this. Cut off the short piece left sticking toward the bend of the hook.

Next, you will need a loop at the end of your snell. Study figure 11-3 to learn the **perfection**

loop. It is easier than it looks at first. The only secret is to not pull on the small end of the line. That will ruin the knot. Cut the small end off near the knot.

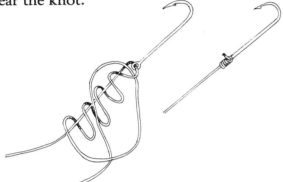

Figure 11-1. Improved clinch knot

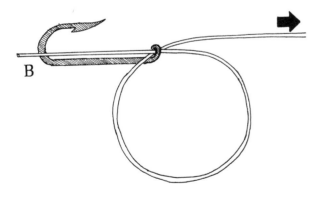

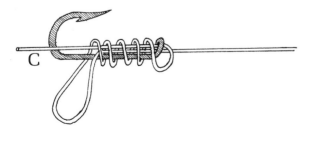

Figure 11-2a, b, c, d. Snelling a hook

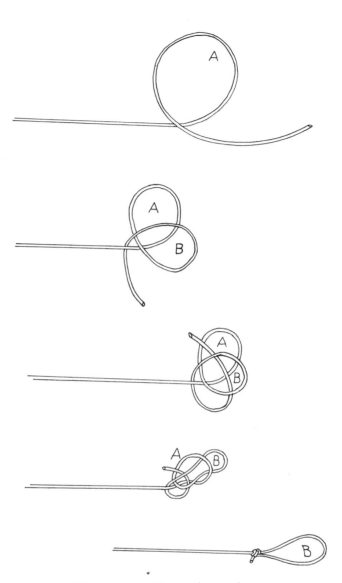

Figure 11-3. The perfection loop

Now that you have a snelled hook with a perfection loop at the end, tie the same loop on the end of your monofilament line or leader. To attach the two, simply push the line loop through the snell loop (fig. 11-4a) and bring the hook through the line loop (fig. 11-4b). This will unite the two loops (fig. 11-4c,d). It is easy to do and also easy to undo if you want to take the hook off. The only disadvantage of using a snelled hook is the large knot made by joining it with the line. But most fish don't notice anyway.

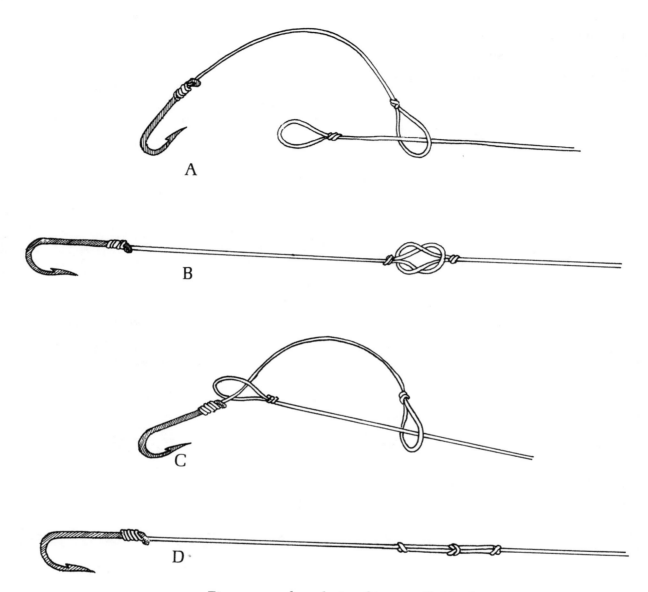

A

B

C

D

Figure 11-4a, b, c, d. Attaching a snelled hook

Because monofilament is so hard and smooth, it is hard to join two pieces together. Yet you have to do this to make tapered leaders (see Chapter 3) or simply to make your leader longer. I will describe two knots that will do this.

The blood knot. Also called barrel knot, this knot is hard to learn but works very well with all kinds of fishing except for very big, strong fish. Figure 11-5 shows how to tie a blood

knot, but it isn't as easy as it looks. One important thing to remember is to make all turns in the same direction. Otherwise it will not work.

Unfortunately, the knot will slip when pulled very hard. I have lost some monster barracuda and other big fish this way. A much stronger knot, and one that is easier to tie, is the surgeon's knot (fig. 11-6). Study this diagram and practice it. It looks confusing at first but if you remember the entire end of the leader passes through the loop, it is simple. The

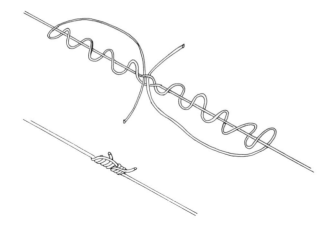

Figure 11-5. The blood knot

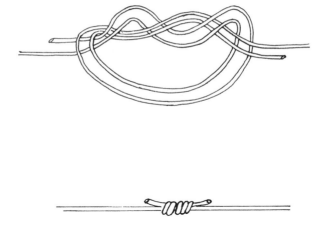

Figure 11-6. The surgeon's knot

resulting knot is a bit lumpy but nearly as strong as the line itself.

The dropper loop. Another important knot to know is the dropper loop. It is used when you want a loop above the end of the line. See below, under rigs, for some of its uses. To tie

it (fig. 11-7), first decide how far in front of the end of the line you want it to be. Then make a loop about two inches wide, with the short end behind the long end (fig. 11-7a). Push the short end through the loop from towards you to away from you. Do this twice (fig. 11-7b). While holding everything in place with your

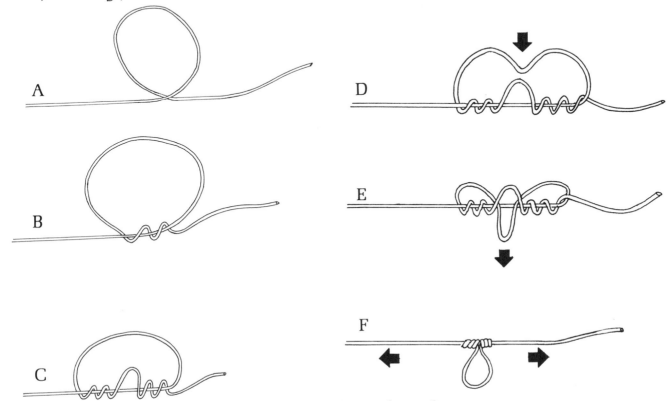

Figure 11-7. Steps in tying a dropper loop

first finger and thumb, put your second finger between the loop and the short end, and push the short end through the loop again, three times (fig. 11-7c). Now you have two loops, the first big one on top and a second one below with your finger in it. Next, pull the large upper loop down through the lower loop (fig. 11-7d). This will take some practice. Tighten the knot by pulling on both ends of the line. This will be easier if you have taken your finger out of the bottom loop and placed it in the upper loop after it is pushed through the bottom loop (fig. 11-7e). Do not pull on the only loop left (the dropper) to tighten it or it won't work. The end result (fig. 11-7f) is a straight line with a perfect loop sticking out one side. You can use this to attach a snelled hook or fly by the method I described above for the perfection loop.

There are several ways to attach a leader to a fly line. Some of these are hard to do, but most fly lines you can buy now have a thin loop at the end that you can attach a leader to in the same way you attach two loops together. Other than this, the **nail knot** is one of the very best

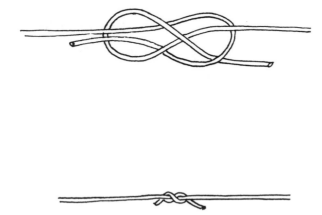

Figure 11-8. The clove hitch

but is a bit too advanced for a beginner. A good substitute is the **clove hitch**. Study figure 11-8 until you have mastered clove hitches. Most fly lines are soft enough that the leader will dig into them and not slip. But if the knot does slip, simply tie an **overhand knot** in the end of the leader (fig. 11-9). An overhand knot will not allow the line and leader to slip apart.

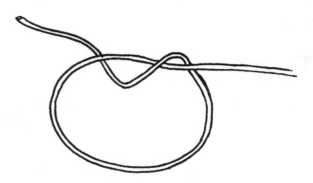

Figure 11-9. A simple overhand knot

Rigs. Hooks, sinkers, leaders, and so forth used in combination are called rigs. There are not many kinds of rigs used in freshwater fishing.

Most bait fishermen use their bait close to the bottom of the lake or stream. Of course, it will take some weight to cast your hook very far, so you will need a sinker. Most people put the sinker above the bait, but before you can feel a bite the fish has to pull the sinker too, which might make your fish pretty suspicious and spit out the bait before you even know that there is a fish in the neighborhood. Instead, tie the sinker on the end of the line with a clinch knot, then use a snelled hook on a dropper loop, as illustrated in figure 11-10. This way, unless the fish swims directly toward you after taking the bait, it will not feel the weight of the sinker and you will have a very sensitive feeling for what is happening.

Another good thing about this rig is that if there are algae and other plants on the bottom of the lake (as there usually are), the bait has a chance to be seen by the fish instead of being buried in the green stuff.

Using a bobber, of course, gets around this problem. You can see when you have a bite when the bobber moves, but on the other hand, the wind will quickly slide your rig in its direction. The wind may take your bait away from the area you want to fish, and will cause your line to "bow," making it difficult to set the hook when you have a bite, because of all of the slack line between you and the bobber. No one ever said fishing is easy!

Figure 11-10. Bait fishing with a dropper loop

No discussion of rigs should omit the highly successful method of using a fly behind a bubble. The bubble (fig. 11-11) should be of clear, colorless plastic with an inner, hollow rod that can be pulled out to allow you to add water for additional weight. Any number of kinds of flies, and even small lures or bait, can be used with this system, usually used with spinning tackle. I usually use two different flies at a time, hoping that at least one will attract a fish. Naturally this requires a dropper loop for the second fly. Simply tie a fly onto a short snell with a clinch knot, attaching it to a dropper loop with a perfection loop. Then, with a fly at the end of the line, you are a double threat to the fish! And if neither fly works it is easy to change flies at either place, using a clinch knot. So, the complete rig looks like figure 11-12. Just behind the bubble is a swivel (or snap-swivel, fig. 11-13), followed by five or six feet of leader carrying one or two flies.

If the fish can be seen feeding near or on the surface (only experience can tell you which), fill the bubble about two-thirds full of water. The bubble will stay just barely on the surface with the flies only a few inches below the surface. Retrieve the bubble slowly with your rod tip close to the surface of the water. When you get a strike, often you can see a swirl in the water behind the bubble even before you feel it. Strike back instantly!

If there is no surface action, that does not mean fish are not feeding. In fact, eating and mating seem to be the things fish are most interested in, like many other animals. In this case, fill the bubble completely with water. After the cast it will slowly sink. When you have decided that it is near the bottom, begin a slow retrieve. You will feel most strikes very clearly, and, by jerking back, you will set the hook. Of

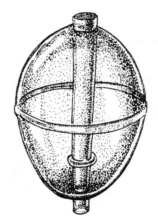

Figure 11-11. A "bubble"

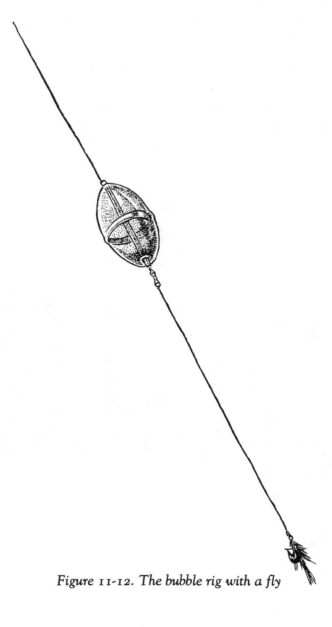

Figure 11-12. The bubble rig with a fly

Figure 11-13. A snapswivel

course, you will catch a lot of weeds too, but that's fishing!

Other rigs are sometimes used for different kinds of fish, or in different kinds of water, but if you learn what I have described so far, you won't have any trouble learning new techniques.

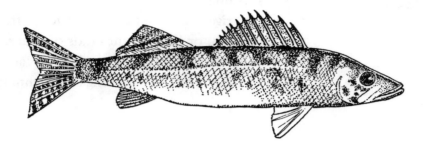

12. How to Clean Fish

Every fisherman, no matter how young or old, has the responsibility of cleaning the catch, so that the fish can be cooked and eaten. It's not a pleasant job, but it can be done quickly if you know how. The basic idea is to get the insides out and the scales or skin off. You will need a sharp knife for this, so use it with care. Of course, you should not cut up a live fish, so be sure it is dead first. If it is not, two or three hard blows to the top of its head with a stick or rock, just behind the eyes, will kill it quickly.

It is very important that your fish are taken care of properly in the time between when you catch them and when you clean them. Fish spoil very quickly. The best way is to keep them alive until you are ready to clean them. This is not always possible, depending on the kind of fishing you are doing, but sometimes it is no problem. If you are fishing from a boat, you can use a wire basket made to hold live fish over the side. This is very good. Or, you can use a stringer, which is a wire or fabric line with a point on one end to push over the fish's gills from behind and out its mouth. The back end of this kind of stringer has a cross piece that

keeps the fish from slipping off. A better stringer is the kind with big snaps or clips that you can attach to the fish without damaging its gills as much as the simple stringer.

The second best technique for keeping fish fresh is to put the fish on ice as soon as possible. Crushed ice or cubes are much better than a block, as the cold air is more evenly distributed. Water from melted ice should be drained off regularly, as fish get soggy and spoil quickly in warm water. Never let fish float around in water, not even in the lake, after the fish have died. Instead, clean them and place them on ice as soon as possible or they will develop a very bad flavor.

Different kinds of fish are cleaned somewhat differently. For example, some are skinned and others are not. Let's start with the outside and work our way in.

Fish with large, soft scales are easily scaled. This means the scales are scraped off with a knife, spoon, or a fish scaler (fig. 12-1). Examples of fish needing scaling are crappie, sunfish, bass, and carp. Simply scrape the skin from the tail towards the head and watch the scales fly! You probably will want to do this outside of

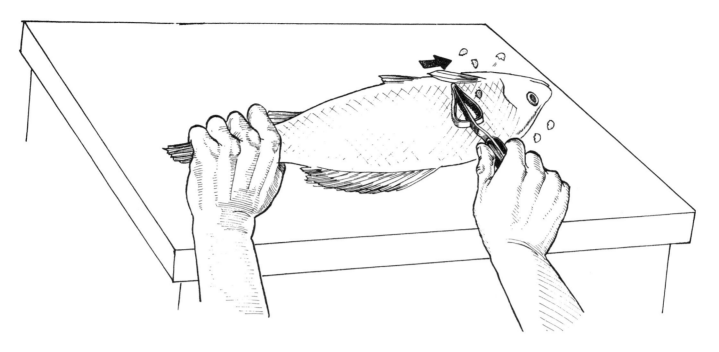

Figure 12-1. Using a fish scaler

the house. If you are scaling a lot of fish, a garden hose with the water on its most powerful stream works nicely to remove scales. But be sure to hang on to your fish or it may end up in the neighbor's yard!

Some fish with scales, such as perch and walleye, are very much attached to their scales so that scraping them is a long, hard job. It is best to peel the skin off such fish. This also is true

of catfish, that have no scales at all, only a tough, slimy skin.

To skin a fish you need a very sharp knife (or even a single-edge razor blade) and a pair of pliers. First cut off the head (fig. 12-2). You may want to make the cut so that it includes the pectoral fins as well, because there is not much meat in that area.

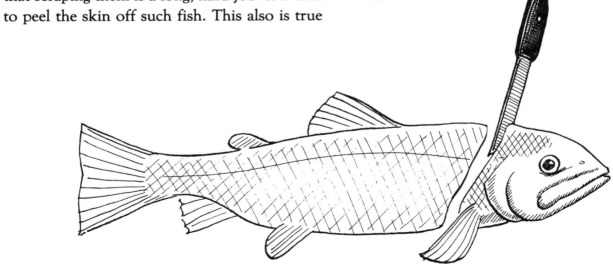

Figure 12-2. Cutting off a fish's head, along with its pectoral fins

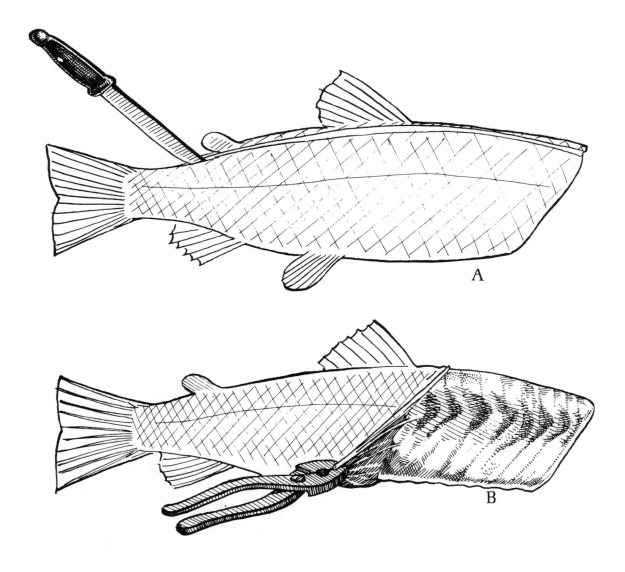

Figure 12-3a, b. Skinning a fish

Holding the fish with its back up, make slices through the skin along the middle, from the front past both sides of the dorsal fin (fig. 12-3a). Then use the pliers to grab one side of the skin and pull it backwards (fig. 12-3b). Usually the entire side will come off in one or two pieces. Then do the other side. As always, be careful of the sharp spines, especially of catfish. After the fish is skinned, the dorsal and anal fins can be pulled out easily with pliers.

Most people do not scale trout because their scales are so small, and it is almost impossible to skin them because the muscles are so tightly attached to the skin. Trout can be filleted, as described below, or the skin can be removed during cooking.

Now that your fish is scaled or skinned, the next step is to get the insides out. This is not time to be squeamish because fish mainly have the same kinds of insides as we do, and they can be very interesting and instructive, as I will describe below.

Turn your fish belly up. You will see its anus (also called vent) just in front of the anal fin.

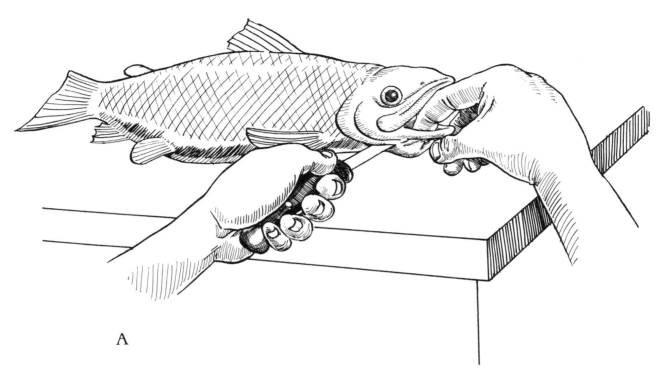

A

Figure 12-4a, b. Beginning to gut a trout

This is the bottom opening of the digestive system, or gut. Push your knife into it and cut forward until the entire body cavity is opened. With your fingers, pull out all of the contents of the body cavity. Rinse it out. Notice the dark mass up against the top of the body cavity. This mass is actually the two kidneys and can be scraped away with a finger or a knife blade. After another rinse your fish is cleaned.

Traditionally, trout are cleaned with the head left on. It certainly is not necessary, but they do look pretty when you bring them home this way. The technique for cleaning trout is simple (fig. 12-4a, b). Push the tongue down with one finger, forming a bulge in the "throat." Slip the knife blade through the skin, under the bulge (look out for your finger) and out the other side of the bulge. Slit forward to release the tongue in a V-shaped cut. Lay down the knife (don't forget to pick it up later—I have knives

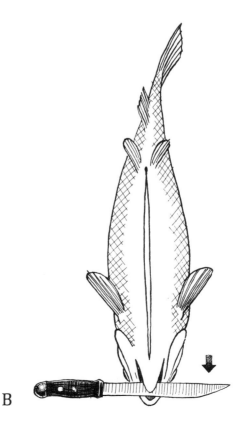

B

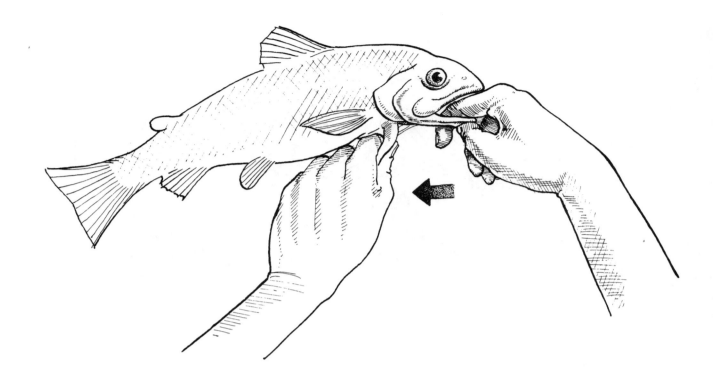

Figure 12-5. Pulling out the internal organs of a trout

scattered across the world), push your first finger on top of the tongue from the bottom cut, and pull everything you can backwards. Be careful of the teeth on top of the tongue. This should tear the tongue, gills, and guts out with one simple action (fig. 12-5). Rinse, scrape out the kidneys, and you have a beautiful, cleaned trout ready to cook. When you have learned to do it, the entire operation should take only a few seconds.

Now, all that we have described leaves you with fish still containing their bones. If you just want the two sides of meat you may wish to fillet the fish. This also takes a little practice and is best done on larger fish with their heads still on. With a very sharp knife make a cut on one side of the fish from just behind the head to behind the pectoral fin. Of course, you will not need to scale the fish first, as the skin will be removed when you are done. Slice the side

off of the fish by cutting backward toward the tail, keeping the sharp edge of the knife scraping against the backbone as you go. When the fillet is cut off, turn the fish over and repeat the operation on the other side. It is easy to cut off the ribs by sliding the knife behind them. Remember that some fish such as pike, trout, carp, and suckers have extra bones, so when you eat them be careful. Some can be removed with a knife when you are filleting the fish. Cut off the belly meat and throw it away, as it is fatty and usually bad tasting. The dorsal and anal fins have sharp internal bones too. Some may be in the cooked meat, so be careful.

To cut off the skin, start at the back end and cut forward as close to the skin as possible. Some fish have a layer of dark brown muscle on each side which is usually bad tasting. This can be cut off, but is removed more easily when you are eating the fish.

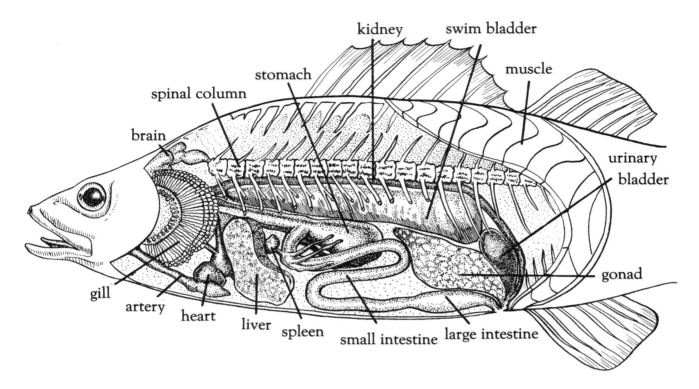

Figure 12-6. A dissected perch, showing its internal organs

Large fish such as big trout, salmon, and walleye can be cut into steaks. Simply cut off the tail and then cut up the fish crossways into pieces about one inch thick. These are delicious when grilled. But don't try it with small fish or the pieces will fall through the grill onto the charcoal.

All fish should be cooked within a day or two, or else frozen for later use. They should never be left at room temperature for more than a few hours because they will spoil very quickly.

I include here a drawing of a perch with its organs in place inside the body (fig. 12-6). Every fisherman should know the internal as well as the external parts of a fish. For example, if you know what the stomach looks like, you can cut it open to see what the fish has been feeding on. This may help you to catch more fish by switching to a bait or fly of the same type as the real dinner.

13. How to Cook Fish

People have been cooking and eating fish for thousands of years, so naturally there are thousands of recipes for cooking them. In fact, many books have been written on the subject. There are three basic techniques: frying, baking, and grilling. I will give you the directions for each of these. After you have tried them you can explore the cooking of fish for the rest of your life.

Frying. Frying a fish takes only a pan with some cooking oil in it. Set the stove at medium, or about 350°, and add cooking oil about one-eighth inch deep. If you are cooking small fish or fillets you would probably like to coat them with flour, cornmeal, bread crumbs, potato buds, or smashed cornflakes before frying them. Add salt and pepper to the coating.

An easy way to coat fish is to put the flour into a paper bag. Then add the fish, close the top of the bag and shake it to cover the fish. Of course, you can buy already prepared mixtures for this, but making your own is more fun.

After the oil is hot, add the fish. It should take only three or four minutes on each side of the fish to cook it well. Test it with a fork. If the flakes of meat come apart easily and the flesh is white, not clear, it is done. Lift them out of the pan with a spatula, onto a plate with paper towels on it. This will soak up much of the oil and make the fish better to eat. Fried fish is very tasty.

If you are young and have not done much cooking before, you should not cook with oil by yourself. Hot oil is very dangerous. I know a person who spilled hot oil on her leg when she was very young and she still has a very big scar where it landed. Do not cook without adult supervision.

Baking. Baking fish is even easier than frying them. Wipe the fish dry with paper towels. Then lay them on a sheet of aluminum foil. Add salt, pepper, and whatever sounds good to you. Many people add a couple of slices of onion, a little sliced lemon, some cooking oil, and perhaps a few teaspoons of milk or cream (fig. 13-1). Wrap up the foil tightly so it won't lose its steam inside, and cook it in the oven at 325°, or on the charcoal broiler. Charcoal broiling and campfire cooking are a bit more difficult because the heat is not constant.

Figure 13-1. Wrapping a fish in foil before baking it

When you are camping you can pan fry your catch or bake it over open coals in the fire. An important thing to remember is to let the fire die down until there are hardly any flames left, but there are lots of red-hot coals. Place your pan or the aluminum-wrapped fish on the coals or a portable grill. Turn the fish over three or four times. When you guess that the fish might be done, carefully open up the foil and see if a fork will easily separate the muscles. If not, put it back for a while.

Grilling. Grilling fish (fig. 13-2), either on a charcoal broiler or an open campfire, can produce a delicious result. Most fish take no special treatment, but trout and salmon are special cases because they are very oily, as are eels. Other species are dry, such as perch, sunfish, bass, and pike. Fatty fish are best cooked on a grill. Excess oil boils out onto the grill and the fish becomes drier.

Any fish can be cooked this way, but let's start with trout. I cut off the head, then split the fish along its length from the bottom side. Af-

ter drying the fish with a paper towel, lay it onto the hot grill with the skin side down. Coat the upper side with the sauce described below. After about one minute, turn it over with a spatula. Grasp the skin at the front end and pull it off. If it is cooked, it will pull off easily.

I prefer to put a sauce on both sides of the meat as it is cooking. My favorite sauce for trout is a mixture of a small amount of Worcestershire Sauce, an equal amount of butter, and some garlic powder. Brush this on the meat as it cooks. Cook the fish until it is done; I prefer to overcook it somewhat so that it is a bit dry. The same method will work on any kind of fish, but don't overcook the drier types of fish.

You will have great fun cooking and eating your own catch. And right away you will begin looking for more ways to cook them, which is part of the fun of fishing.

Figure 13-2. Grilling a fish

14. Fishing Ethics

Ethics are the rules we live by to improve our lives and the lives of others. In fishing, we must follow rules to improve the quality of fishing and to make ourselves better people to be with. Some ethical things are enforced by law, such as how many fish you can take in a day. Others are more personal, and depend on our sense of responsibility to enforce. For example, you won't go to jail for leaving your trash behind, but certainly it is not an ethical thing to do. Other people will not enjoy themselves as much if you leave a lot of junk behind. Neither would you, so why do it?

I have no intent of telling you how to live your life, but I will list a few things that make the difference between being a true fisherman and a slob.

Always know the laws that apply to where you are fishing. Every state has free copies of rules that you must read and follow. This is not just to keep you from paying fines or even going to jail, but to help preserve our fishing for ourselves, our children, and for generations of fishermen to come.

Never litter the area with trash. If you bring things in, carry them out. Pop cans, for exam-

ple, will last a lifetime and look terrible on the beach of a lake or river. Paper and other things might eventually decompose but they should be carried out, too. Don't bury your trash because animals may just dig it up and spread it around. Always carry your trash out.

When you gut a fish outdoors near where you caught it, bury the guts in the sand. Never leave trout heads exposed or feed them to gulls or other fish-eating birds, as parasites in the eyes of trout will be spread around to infect even more trout, making them blind. This is actually a law in some states.

Fishline is one of the worst things you can leave behind. A bunch of it can not only tangle up someone else's tackle, but also can wrap around birds' legs, fish's heads, and muskrats' legs, and cause them a horrible death. Never throw monofiliment lines or leaders on the ground. Carry them out in your pocket.

Consider barbless hooks in your fishing. You can buy them barbless, or simply flatten the barb down with pliers. I don't lose any more fish with barbless hooks than with those that have barbs, and it is so much easier to release a fish with little damage to its delicate tissues

when the hook has no barb that it seems silly not to fish this way.

Another aspect of fishing with barbless hooks to consider is with spoons and other lures. Usually these come attached with treble hooks—three barbed hooks melted together. I have removed the treble hooks from the lure, replaced them with single hooks, and found I catch as many fish. And the fish do not have to suffer your attempts at pulling out three hooks instead of one.

Never trespass on someone's property. Often, if you ask permission, a landowner will allow you to cross the property. If you do not get permisson, remember that land owners have the right to control who uses their land. Trespass laws vary from state to state and country to country. In one area it may be legal for you to walk along a river a certain distance from the water, while in another area it may even be illegal to wade the river bed. Know the laws where you fish and respect the property of others.

It is very rude to fish too close to another fisherman without being invited. For example, if someone is sitting beside a lake and is catching a lot of fish, don't plop yourself down right there. It is OK to ask what bait, lures, or flies are working, and if he is considerate, he will tell you. Unfortunately, some fishermen seem to think that they are competing against the rest of the world to see who can catch the most fish. But, if I am doing well with a certain pattern of fly, I will happily give one to whomever asks what I am using. It is much better to make a new friend than to make a stranger mad at you.

If you walk up to a river, be sure you do not start to fish right above someone. Either move a good distance upstream or go back down-

stream to fish. Even if the fish have been scared, they have short memories and will begin feeding again soon. Also, if the river is crowded, don't spend all day in a choice place. You should keep moving ahead so that someone else has a chance.

If you are trolling from a boat, be sure not to get too close to bank fishermen. You might tangle your line with theirs. Always respect another person's space. This is true no matter what you are doing.

Remember, fishing should be fun, not a competition between you and anyone else. Its most important aspect is to put you close to the nature you are a part of, helping you realize your place in the Universe.

Index